Caller No. 5

Elizabeth Blackwood

This one goes out to all you *Brads* out there.

Chapter One

The wind knocked the ashes of Kat Walker's cigarette onto her sun-freckled forearm. She kicked the habit often, but a thousand times and it rolled back downhill like a snowball headed for hell.

She brushed ashes away and tightened her crimson-manicured grip on the steering wheel and her emerald gaze on the road. Wispy bleach blonde hairs escaped her loose ponytail as her Jaguar F-Type ran like a scalded dog along the spine of the Cowrock ridge that belonged to the Blue Ridge section of the Appalachian mountains.

The moonlight overhead stained the landscape in ghost forms, and only two sounds could be heard for miles around, the convertible's engine and the music that wailed into the hushed mountainside.

The stars seemed to drip down from the velvet night sky and splay themselves across her windshield as the disc jockey of 105.3 *The Love Line* purred out to all listeners.

105.3 broadcasted all varieties of music based on caller requests and local news and weather.

105.3 The top station in the nation for the sounds you know and love.

She hadn't called into the station tonight. Usually, Kat would call in and talk to the Love Doctor and he would play her a song. Somehow it always helped, the Love Doctor would know exactly what to play.

Love had never worked out for Kat.

At least, not how it worked in the movies or even in the songs that she listened to religiously. No man would ever love her enough to let her stay on the door and he froze to death. No, instead he would ride away on a wild horse. No dragging necessary.

She wanted a companion, someone who could understand her and someone who would let her into his mind and not hide any secrets because she never did.

Kat led a very private life outside of her work and the only person she talked to was the Love

Doctor. He always knew what to say to make Kat feel like she had won the lottery. He had never seen her but called her beautiful. She felt she could be herself with the Love Doctor even on air with thousands of listeners horning in every time.

She wasn't big or small, but somewhere in the middle. She wasn't short or tall, she was average. She was quiet, kept to herself, and relied more on the teachers' advice than the guidance of her peers.

There wasn't anything special about Kat Walker.

Not to her or to anybody else.

She enjoyed driving at night with the top down and radio on screaming the lyrics to her favorite songs and casting her worries to the wind.

In high school she never had friends. After all, she couldn't invite them to the squalor of her home for a bubbly slumber party fueled by sugar, teen magazines, and exclusive boy talk.

Not in her home.

She never won awards or recognition for anything. She didn't join in during pep rallies and she didn't provide much for school spirit.

Kat had been a B student who missed so much school the truant office had visited their dilapidated home numerous times in failed attempts to speak to her father.

Her father was a raging alcoholic after her mother packed up and left, tired of dealing with overdue bills that began to pile up as her father had managed his shade tree mechanic shop.

He tinkered with people's vehicles and lawnmowers. Somehow he paid the bills and had enough left over to buy a case of beer each day.

Kat would babysit the neighborhood kids while their parents went out on the weekends or after school until they got off work. It wasn't much money, but it helped with groceries, buying second-hand clothes at the salvage barn, and a time or two had helped turn the power back on. It also paid for those golden tickets to the Friday night games where she could root on Brad Turner who had made Varsity Quarterback their senior year.

Brad had never shown much interest in Kat aside from when he cracked jokes with his friends or his girlfriend Sidnie Chancellor, Captain of the Cheerleading Squad. Kat felt he was pressured to do so by Sidnie, his cohorts, and peers because in private, when no one was around, he talked to her and she'd listen.

She would watch him as if he hung the moon as he complained about how the coach had pushed them so brutally at practice until they puked and would refuse them water.

He confided in Kat about Sidnie's unfaithfulness to him and how often she had cheated on him with his good buddies and even the coach. She *oohed* and *aahed* while she listened to the stories of his agility on the field and the touchdown he scored right before the game was over and won them the season his sophomore year. Brad would grin and the smile would reach his sparkly, baby-blue eyes right over his broken-too-many-times-but-still- handsome nose. She would move subconsciously under his piercing gaze.

He talked to her until that Thursday night.

After her father had drunk himself into a stupor in front of the TV, Brad came over to talk. He parked his Range Rover a few houses down in front of the old dry cleaner store where they'd usually sit and make out while her father slept off his drink. That night he'd gone through the trouble of getting his older brother to buy some liquor from the local package store a town over since they lived in a dry county.

Kat would drink the warm beer after her father passed out and would have to pry the can from his grip. She could maybe get away with a single cold one from the fridge. Maybe. No matter how polluted her father became, he was still very keen on his inventory. One might go unnoticed, but two was one too many.

She'd never tried that liquor that Brad poured from a bottle wrapped in a brown paper sack. He filled them both a shot on the dashboard and they clinked the glasses and threw them back.

Kat gasped as the liquid fire washed down her throat. Brad had gotten a kick out of it and quickly poured a second and pushed it into her hand. By the time she had swallowed down her fourth shot, she felt the full effects of the spirits coursing like lava through her body.

Brad made sexual advances. He'd try to slide his hands beneath her shirt or between her legs and Kat would push him away and he'd get frustrated and leave her standing at the empty dry cleaners alone in the night. Sometimes she'd just give in and let go. It wouldn't last long and then he'd leave after he made some derogatory comment about her ratty clothes or how she had gained weight.

That night and that time he wouldn't get frustrated and leave. He pulled at her blouse, the fabric so threadbare from age and time-worn and occasionally washed in the high-powered industrial machines at the laundromat. It ripped like tissue paper in his hands. She had fled the vehicle as he chased Kat to her front door and into her home and there on the dirty stained rug of the kitchen floor he pinned her down, alcohol heavy on his breath as he whispered in her ear.

"C'mon, Kitty Kat. I've got a big game tomorrow night and that bitch is screwing the other team's lineman. A lineman, Kat. L-listen to me, babe. I ain't gonna tell nobody. It's me and you, here.

Your dad won't hear us. I'm with *you*."

The ghost of a lie long since passed.

Kat belted the words along with Blondie's "One Way or Another" and drummed her fingers enthusiastically along with the rhythm on the steering wheel as she flipped her blinker up and pulled to the shoulder of the road. She killed the engine while the radio and blinker remained on, its faint flash lit up the lonesome wilderness around the Jaguar.

Kat got out of the vehicle, rested against it, and then lit a cigarette from a tin metal case she'd picked up a few towns back. She took a long drag, and exhaled, her breath fading out before her in the air. The moon above was almost full as she popped open the Jaguar's trunk and the white light spilled inside onto the body of Brad Turner, football star and dream boy 101. Too bad he didn't play football anymore. He had been really doing it out there as the top quarterback at Sugardale High.

Now, the only time he held a football was when he pushed it across the barcode at the register of Jerry Jenerals, or as some people called it JJ's.

It was difficult getting a body in the trunk of her Jaguar and even more so when trying to get one out. Kat found it more simple to use the weight of the corpse to her advantage and simply dump it into the trunk like a big sack of potatoes. Work smarter, not harder.

A fresh body like this one is very limp, the muscles not yet riddle with Rigour mortis, and would settle well in the bottom of the cargo area. She thought it kind of reminded her of getting her shoe stuck in the mud, easy to get in there and hard to get out.

Finally, she managed to pull Brad free from the Tupperware container that was the trunk he had rested in for over a hundred miles. He groaned when his torso hit the ground. She struggled with his ungainly body and dragged it towards the yellow NO ENTRY signs of Lovers Gulch.

Lovers Gulch was a pocket of canyon that wound around a grove of natural Georgia pines. It had been a community landmark among the small towns that surrounded these parts and even included a gentle stream and a waterfall. However, as times have passed and people found themselves inside their homes and inside the screens of their new friends on social media, places like Lovers Gulch have become obsolete.

There was trash everywhere and the stone benches had been broken, pushed over, and covered in graffiti. What looked like a bicycle was thrown into the stream with the trash and debris. The ancient pines had the bark stripped halfway up the trees and along the creamy trunk were the names of thousands of visitors carved into their flesh "M+P=4EVR", "YOLO", "Vegas or Bust".

She dragged Brad along the littered trail full of broken beer bottles and used needles and condoms. She stopped to catch her breath and Brad let out a whimper. Kat puffed on her cigarette and examined Brad. He didn't move much and couldn't. His hands and feet were bound with twelve feet of rope, gagged with his own socks, and drugged. Her drug of preference was classic, chloroform, bleach, and rubbing alcohol.

One whiff of her handkerchief knocked this one-hundred-and-eighty-pound, washed-up all-star on his back. She lifted her foot and smooshed a pink tennis shoe into his cheek. Brad had a gash on his forehead above his right eye that had gushed after his head had hit the coffee table in his living room. Now, it was crusted over in blood. His weight had also knocked the table over along with the candles, white wine, and strawberries she had set up for him while he was at work.

Poor Brad worked all the time at a dead-end job and never had time for Kat. When he came home he would take a shower and then sit in front of the TV until he fell asleep. His meals consisted of carryout and pizza. He never cooked so Kat prepared a meal just for him. She surprised him with a delicious banquet with all of his favorite dishes. She even made a dessert of crème brûlée. When Brad made it home he was so surprised by what Kat did for him that he tried to run.

"What did you do to me?" Brad's voice came out so slurred and garbled through his Jerry Jenerals brand socks she held over his mouth and his sloth-like body squirmed against his bonds.

His black JJ's uniform was torn and covered in dirt, leaves, and trash from being dragged on the ground of Lovers Gulch trail. Kat kicked Brad in his ribs and continued to drag him towards the stream. The stream fed the waterfall down into a huge gully that was Lovers Gulch. She dragged Brad towards the edge of the rock facing and rolled him over on his stomach so that his head hung off the cliff. His view was impeccable. Down below he would be able to see the true beauty of Lovers Gulch.

She leaned against a gnarled and scarred-up Pinetree that overhung the gully and took out her cell phone. She dialled the number and listened for the ring. A deep soulful voice answered on the other line and she smiled.

"What's your name darlin'?" the Love Doctor asked.

"It's Kat, from Sugardale, Georgia."

She brushed her hair out of her face and primped her 105.3 t-shirt that she'd gotten from another previous call-in. It had a screen print of a heart with two band-aids crossed over a crack in the center and the station name captioned below.

"Uh-oh folks, looks like we got some Sugar on the line. Miss Sugardale, is a regular to the theraputicities of the Love Doctor. Kat, you are Caller No. 1. What is your question for the Love Doctor tonight?"

"Well," Kat sighed.

"Well, that's a deep subject you've found yourself in Sugar. What's happening with that man in your life? Is he still not doing what you want him to do? Is he not listening to what you have to say? Don't let him walk all over you, Sugar." The Love Doctor's voice rang out on speakerphone through the canyon and was swallowed by the waterfall's steady rush.

"No, he's not. Try as I might, he's stubborn and won't move." She kicked Brad and then took a seat on his back.

"He doesn't listen to what I have to say LD. All he does is sleep and he called me names tonight. Like not my real name, bad ones." Her fingers played with the torn fibers of his uniform, his shallow breaths puffed up small dust devils at her side.

"Man, that's not how you treat a lady, is it fella's?" The Love Doctors crew hooted and hollered on the phone's speaker. "Now, Sugar, you need you a *real* man, one to hold you, to kiss you, to love you all night long and the next day. Drop that zero and get you a hero. You know love is a strange and beautiful thing and it takes patience. Next up is "Patience" by Guns N' Roses. Kat from Sugardale?"

"Yes, LD?" She said eagerly into the phone. She looked at the black screen with 105.3's number at the top.

"How about I hook you up with a free t-shirt for calling tonight? Just stay on the line and give Darnell your information. Good luck, Sugar. The Love Doctor will be on call. Goodnight." She took the last cigarette from her pack in between her lips and tossed the empty box into the gulley. The chloroform was starting to wear off as Brad made more noises and coughed against his gag. He moaned as Kat pushed herself to stand and he wailed when his eyes focused below. His face was red and flushed as he hung over the side. He cried and attempted to maneuver his way out from his restraints. To no avail, he couldn't pull loose, but only tightened the knots. His muscles were taxed from being drugged, dragged, starved, and shut up in the trunk for hours on end. He spit out his socks and looked around until he managed to see Kat standing over him.

"It's *you*. You Nutty Bitch. You come into JJs all the time and…you were in my house! How did you-Who are you? People know about you, they've seen you talking to me. They'll know it was you!" He spit in her direction.

"Oh, Brad, why do you have to say such things about me? I do everything I can for you and it's not enough. It's never enough."

"You listen here, you crazy fucking bitch, let me go." Brad's baby blues were bloodshot and beneath the blood-rushed hue, his complexion was sheet white.

"Brad, I don't like the way you are talking to me. If it hadn't been for your daddy paying the board you wouldn't have made the grades to even play football."

"What are you talking about? I'm not Brad! My name is Aaron! Aaron Michaels. I don't even play sports anymore. I'm not Brad!"

"So many lies, Brad. You know what you did to me and then what you spread across the school. My father beat me until I couldn't walk because of your lies. No one would believe me. Lying isn't good for proper digestion. Have you eaten yet, Brad? Yes? Well, you shouldn't eat before you swim. You might get a cramp and you could drown." Kat chided him as if he were a child going to play in the pool. He struggled to kick at Kat as she removed his shoes again and threw them one at a time into the water, far down below, and then with a solid push Brad's top heavy body lurched and slid over the side.

Kat picked her way back to the roadside where her Jaguar was parked, the blinker still flashed repeatedly, and her favorite disc jockey spilled his love into the ears of his listeners and fans.

"This is the Love Doctor, wishing all you hopeful romantics out there to find love and have a good ol' time. Who knows Caller No.1 could be the woman of your dreams."

Chapter Two

Deputy Sheriff Busby Ballard patrolled the downtown streets of Pucket, Georgia. Puckett was located on the state line of Georgia and Tennessee and rested on a slope of a mountain overlooking the valley below. There wasn't much to the town and most folks bypassed it on the new highway heading to the bigger cities with outlet centers and fancy restaurants. Founded by Jeremiah Puckett in the early 1900s, it had once been a big tourist site with vendors in the main street village selling all kinds of memorabilia on the private towns' scenic views.

Now, there wasn't much to patrol in Puckett which meant that Deputy Bus could do a full sweep of the town in about an hour while driving his confiscated golf cart. He was a short-statured guy and had the mindset of a Chihuahua who thought he was a Mastiff. Most people laughed at him when he pulled them over in his squad cart, but weren't so happy later when they showed up on their court day for their particular violations with notarized subpoenas in hand. The sides of his electric vehicle had bright blue mailbox lettering that spelled out LCPD, "Line County Police Department ".

Deputy Bus did the cart detailing himself and even set up a little side business for decals. It wasn't a lucrative business since the town had shut down and hid inside itself.

Many of the dirty jobs that none of the other boys in blue wanted to do came directly to Bus. Bucky would get a call in and Bus would be on the job immediately, nipping the situation in the bud. One of the dirtiest duties Bus was relied upon to complete was parking duty. By the end of each day, Bus could wrack up almost four parking violations alone. Sometimes the perpetrators would escape the old cart and he'd have to call it in. Good thing he could memorize license plates so easily because he had to keep the streets clean. It was his duty as the Deputy Sheriff of Line County and as the kin of Sheriff Bucky Ballard to keep them as pristine as possible. He had a lot of responsibility on his shoulders and sometimes the weight of his badge became too much, but if he didn't do it then somebody else would and Bus didn't like that idea at all. He was capable of catching anything Line County hurled toward his proficient face.

During high school, Bucky looked out for Bus. Bucky was a year older than Bus so they had been placed in different grades. Bucky had been quite popular in high school and had been a part of everything. If Bucky was there then so was Bus, the two were inseparable.

Bus's nickname was *Short Bus*.

He'd been picked upon by the seniors and sophomores, even members of the Chess Club. He loathed chess, it was too easy, and no one could handle losing to Bus.

They were jealous.

Bus remembered what Bucky always said.

"If someone's mean to you, then they are just jealous, Bus. You can't hold any of their words in your hands, they ain't nothing."

Parking in his assigned place in front of Floyd's Diner, Bus looked into the mirror of his squad cart at his own reflection. He didn't look like anyone around this town. It had always bothered him but his parents and Bucky had reminded him how special that actually was. Everyone strived so hard to be different and look different these days and Bus didn't have to work at it. It came naturally.

This morning there had been a strenuous patrol and Bus was famished. He straightened his badge when his heart felt it was about to burst with pride at the memory of his cousin's honest words. Their words couldn't be held in his hands, and they couldn't be seen either. He took his hat off and smoothed down his cowlick as he exited his squad cart. He pulled up his pants and shined up his big, shiny LCPD belt buckle he'd received after seven years on the force. It was just another one of the perks of being a strong arm of the law.

The cowbell attached to the door rattled as Bus pushed it open and sunlight spilled into the dimly lighted diner that was Floyd's. The diner had a bar with five wooden stools pushed up tightly against the counter and four booths along the walls. Two stools at the counter were occupied by some regulars, although not directly sitting next to each other. Bus sidled up to the barstool in the middle of the two regs and dinged the bell for the waitress. About the time he rang the bell a redhead appeared behind them and placed a slice of peach pie in front of the man to Bus's left. Maryanne turned her attention to Bus as she sucked the gooey peach pie filling off of her thumb.

"Now Bus, I know you like ringing that darn bell, but you knew I was comin'. I hear that thing enough with these two keepin' the stools warm all day and worn out. DP over here is propping him up with his stick." She picked with customers and poked as she patted Bus on the back and took out a pad and pencil from her waist apron and Bus chattered off his order. Her powder blue dress uniform was pressed and she looked magnificent in it.

Doyle Poindexter, the dark-skinned man to Bus's right was drinking down a tall glass of JJ's cola and eating his own piece of pie. When Bus finished giving his order to Maryanne, Doyle was slurping down the final drops of cola and then shook the ice in his empty glass to catch Maryanne's attention.

When Maryanne walked over to get Doyle's glass he gave her powder blue bottom a firm swat and barraged her with dubious questions.

"Can I get a coffee now, ma'am? Have you got any of that cake from yesterday? Nobody wants it now, it's old, right? You throwin' it out, Miss Maryanne?" His voice was a wheeze on a whine with a side of pity. For a grown man of sixty-five, he sure wanted to be treated like a child and wanted everything free of charge.

"Now, Doyle if I catch you layin' hands on Miss Maryanne I think I'm goin' to have to take you in for harassment. I got a nice cot ready for you. You want to know what's on the menu for tonight. It ain't peach pie."

Doyle put his hands up and shook his head and then removed himself from the counter, his whittled walking stick in his hands as he hobbled over to a booth near the front window.

Maryanne brought Doyle an empty cup and filled it full of the dark bean brew. She swapped the empty sugar bowl on Doyle's table with the table beside its full one and returned to the kitchen where she and Granny Flora were creating Bus's masterpiece.

The man to Bus's left was Michael McDonald, he was always rather quiet and merely drank cup after cup of black coffee. He never got cream or sugar so he only had to pay twenty-five cents a cup. He owned most of the land and properties in Line County and often came to Floyd's and talked to the other gents who stopped for a bite to eat. Always prospecting and searching to buy up all the property he could get his hands on. He had more perks than Bus, but not when it came to belt buckles and lunch. His other relatives had long ago sold off their estate and now lived on a beach somewhere. Besides being a large proprietor in Puckett, he was the town's Mayor as well as a judge for the past thirty-seven years.

Bus always imagined sitting in his seat and pounding the gavel and saying *No, you're out of order. Guilty as charged!*

Bus had already missed breakfast this morning and it was almost lunchtime now, just another sacrifice he made every day for his fellow citizens of Line County. Maryanne reappeared and laid his feast before him, pancakes, heavy on butter and syrup. Granny Flora even created a smiley face with the chocolate chip pieces. Sometimes he'd see her talking to Mr. McDonald and would be so upset when he left the diner. Ever since his momma got sick he saw him visit more often. Bus prided himself on his observation skills. It came in handy while soliciting citations for all those parking violations and getting every question right on the radio, but he never called in before. He kind of had a slight speech impediment he had been picked on relentlessly for, but Maryanne said it was endearing. She liked it and she was the foxiest lady in town.

With a mouth full of chocolate chip pancakes and drippy syrup Bus called to the waitress. "Maryanne, when are you gonna let me take you out on the town? I know a little place down the road that we could eat at some time. The food is really good. Daddy won't mind setting another plate at all. C'mon, what do you say?" He pulled a wad of napkins from the holder and wiped at the syrup that ran down his stubbled chin. He missed some and Maryanne wiped it off with a napkin.

"You wouldn't have to cook anything. He won't mind at all." Bus assured her through a mouthful of pancakes and syrup.

The waitress giggled as she filled up his glass of chocolate milk again. She'd eventually give in. Maryanne wouldn't be able to resist Bus's manliness and austere advances. Women loved a man in uniform. He really liked Maryanne Jenkins, she didn't treat Bus like a normal police officer. When she talked to him he felt like a normal guy. He was after all, even when he took his badge off at night to take a bubble bath. He wasn't all laws and regulations, he was just a man looking for the right woman.

He finished his mound of pancakes, downed his third glass of chocolate milk, and dug into his pocket for a wadded-up George Washington, and dropped it on his sticky plate.

"Now, you boys take it easy on Miss Maryanne. If they give you any trouble at all, you just call me on that walkie-talkie I gave you. I've got it on the right channel so don't worry about tuning it." Bus pushed the door open into the mountain town. From across town the bell of the church rang solemnly, serving as both a bell ringing for a mass gathering of searching souls and for one garnering the students and educators of Pucket Academy of Religious Arts and Science formerly known as The Little Red Schoolhouse, somehow the two schools of thought had found a middle ground.

Lunchytime for the kiddos, and time for another sweep of old Puckett.

Bus sat in the squad cart and fiddled with his small, red, JJ's FM radio he had installed onto the dash with some duct tape, and turned up the volume and tuned the dial for 105.3 The Love Line. He got all his advice for the ladies from the Love Doctor. The Love Doctor was one of the smoothest criminals Bus knew and occasionally called in for advice on his sexploits with the opposite gender, i.e. Maryanne. That hot little vixen was going to be Bus's prisoner of love before long.

The Love Doctor wasn't on call yet, he would sign on later in the evening while Bus was on night watch. Friday through Sunday were as the Love Doctor would say *for the therapucities of the soul.*

Nothing ever happened at night in Puckett, the town became a ghost town, but Bus remained ever vigilant. When the town slept he was their eyes and ears. He put the cart in reverse and then drove forward on his second patrol of the day. The weatherman on the radio called in a perfect forecast for the week but counted the weekends to be a bit on the soggy side.

"Cool temperatures all week long and in the seventies, and heavy showers expected for the weekend, thanks, Bob. Now on recent news, a horrific tragedy has impacted the state of Georgia as multiple bodies have been discovered dotting the Cowrock mountain communities. The bodies of two victims are under forensic analysis and no suspect has been found. Details of the case have yet to be released to the public. Tune in later tonight and we will hear from some of the key witnesses. I'm Natalie Crestburn and this is the twelve o'clock news."

"Well, I'll be." Bus scratched his head.

Dead bodies were found around the Cowrock Range communities. Too close to home.

"Bus. Pick up the walkie. Bus? Over." He heard Bucky's voice crackle over the radio.

He sounds upset.

Bus reached for the walkie strapped to his belt and held the button down to speak.

"Gee, Bucky, did you hear about the bodies on the radio? Over."

"Yeah, Bus, that's what I'm doing right now. I got called down late last night. It's a mess. We've got a body and something else on our hands and no suspect. Over."

"Well, what do you want me to do? I had no idea, nobody told me about it. I don't have gloves, but I can bring you some sandwich baggies. Over."

"Nah, you don't need to come down here, I need you to focus on those parking violators. I'll handle this. Over."

"Alright, but I'll be on standby, baggies on the ready, whenever you need me. Oh. Over."

"I know you will, hold the fort down, Bus. Over and out."

The electric cart slung pea gravel as Bus came around the bend, his blue magnetic light stuck to the top of the squad cart, flashed emphatically. He wasn't going to sit around and let Bucky do all the work. They needed him now more than ever.

The scene before Bus was filled with cars and tents popped up on the roadside. This side of the Cowrock hadn't seen this many people in years. He saw so many parking violations and it took everything inside Bus to not make them use proper parking procedures. But he needed to find Bucky at the moment as he marched into the crowd. He caught glances in his direction and brushed them aside like they had their ability to park a motor vehicle correctly as vehicles were parked haphazardly on the highway.

At the trailhead, there was a group of detectives huddled around something on the ground. They took pictures of a black sock from all angles, picked it up with seven-inch tweezers, and then bagged it. Bus couldn't help but feel like he was in one of his favorite crime TV shows and watching the whole thing go down as he navigated the trail. A brisk downhill walk laden with trash and now littered with tiny flags and caution tape.

Lovers Gulch had once been a popular spot. People used to come and visit the site repeatedly, but it had run down over time with little maintenance and blatant disregard. People were everywhere now in groups as they picked away at the evidence, analyzed their notes, and briefed their superiors. They carefully judged whether something was a piece of trash or hard evidence and that was difficult with the state of the public area.

Bucky was at the far end of the trail where the stream fed the waterfall. He was peering down into the gully where they were hoisting a body from below. Once retrieved, the body was found to be bloated and the flesh flaked away like wet oatmeal from the continuous heat of the spring.

"Good God Almighty, Bucky. Don't he look like one of them puffer fishes?" Bus stood with his hands on his hips as he peered down at the body with his mouth agape just inside of Bucky's right peripheral.

Bucky turned and sidestepped, coming in between Bus and the body.

"Dogonit Bus, I told you to do parking duty. You ain't supposed to do anything, but that today. We've got a gathering tonight to paint the courthouse. Don't know if it's gonna fit the budget. But you need to be in town making sure everyone is parked in the right places."

Sheriff Ballard turned back to face the victim's bloated corpse. He looked to be in his late twenties to early thirties, dressed in a black uniform, but barefoot.

"But Bucky.." Bus was confused. He knew that parking violations came first and foremost, but this was murder to the finest degree. He wanted to be on the case with Bucky.

"Oh, don't you, *but Bucky* me right now, Deputy. You can hang around and jot down anything you see or find out and we'll talk about it back in town, but I've got to get some folks down there to scout the bottom of that gulley." Bucky's eyes went from the body to the gulley, back to the body.

"Lord only knows what's down there. I thought this place had been shut down years ago. It's in a terrible shape. Officer Dumas, ring up the Mayor, I've got some questions I need to go over with him when we get back to town."

While Bucky was busy fishing the puffer fish body from the gulley Bus walked around the various tents and groups of investigators like he was a kid at a carnival. He had questions for everyone about everything. In his hand, he kept his LCPD leather notepad he received from Bucky for his first year on the force. It was still in great condition and had all of the original blank pages. Usually, he never had anything important to write in it, but today was a different kind of day. Nothing like this had ever happened in Puckett or in Line

County to be perfectly exact and he wasn't going to miss out on a single tidbit.

In his cart, he sipped on a warm JJ's cola while rereading his notes. It was well into the afternoon and the sun was setting. The Love Doctor would be on call soon. He needed some professional advice on love for his dear Bus-struck Maryanne. The reporter on the radio chimed in after the brief music break and began to divulge the most recent updates on the Line County murder.

"Dude, I don't even know. Me and my lady were taking a late-night walk, like we normally do, but we didn't realize it was private property. You know, and the next thing we know we find a body. Like for real, a real dead person. Not how I wanted my night to go."

Chapter Three

Sheriff Bucky Ballard studied the bloated corpse of his John Doe as it rested near the edge of the drop-off. Two homicides had been performed with the same drop site for the bodies and different methods were used.

At first glance, the victim looked identical to that of a boiled chicken with a black butcher's twine wrapped around its scrawny wings and legs.

The chicken had been hog-tied with nylon rope and in theory, Bucky believed that the victim had been purposely pantsed prior to being dumped. Possible scenarios plagued his mind. Had the chicken been alive or dead before taking a dive into the hot spring below? But foremost who did it and why? How could this have occurred in his jurisdiction?

The second body found in the gulch's spring bed was indistinguishable as its bare, meatless, water-bogged bones bore no expression or released any detail of an identity. There was no telling how long Jane or Jim had been left on simmer before the spring chicken showed up. The skeleton could have been anchored while the chicken had been a mere dumpling floating atop the bubbling waters. Not only did Bucky have these two enigmas on his hands, but a third in Bear Creek as well.

He hadn't received much information on Bear Creeks since he had arrived at Gulch's site.

Now that he had everyone down here picking up rocks in this mosh pit he would have his answers rise to the top like some alphabet soup message.

Of course, the community center would have to be converted into a crime lab to find out the identity of these victims.

That would be a safe job for Bus to orchestrate.

Bucky had always looked out for Bus and he tried to pull his weight around his Aunt and Uncle's house as they had taken custody and raised him after the death of his parents.

At thirteen years old, Bucky moved into Dorris and Dick Ballard's home. They cared for him in any way they could. Aunt Dorris was in rough shape now and miserable and Dick was a Pharmacist and their home had a room attached at the back where the Pharmacy had been housed. Dick could stay at home and wait for a bell to ring at the pharmacy and go through the back entrance to handle the customers filling or picking up their medications.

Sure, they'd shared a room in the small two-bedroomed house, but Bucky and Bus had never wanted anything and had clothes, books, toys, and love. His Aunt and Uncle had never acted like caring for Bucky had been a burden and as a child, Bucky had been grateful.

Aunt Dorris was a superb cook and always asked Bus to set the plates and utensils out for everyone before they seated themselves. Dick would recite the four-minute blessing from the heart and break the bread each night.

On prom night Uncle Dick even allowed Bucky and Bus to use the family's prized '66 Studebaker he always kept covered up and parked in front of the house. He had been so nervous given so much responsibility that he'd almost forgotten to pick up his and Bus's dates for the night, the Skinner sisters. That had been quite a night for a young boy coming of age.

He'd been with plenty of women in his lifetime, but Bucky had never settled down. He was in his late thirties and figured it was too late to start now.

Sure, he wanted a family, two boys, and a blue-eyed girl. He had never gotten around to building a home for himself and usually slept in the station to get sleep at night. He felt guilty each night for doing so and removing himself from the Bavarian home where his Aunt moaned and wailed into the night in agony. With no one significant to share a home with it seemed an empty dream and haunted him on the long lonely nights in his cell.

Once there was a girl.

One who had made his mind rattle around like a handful of rocks in a tin can. He had been deeply in love with Kari Denny, they had been high school sweethearts, but she had ceased returning Bucky's affections after the miscarriage and developed an itch. She lost grasp with reality and he felt that Kari couldn't any longer grasp the concept of what a real relationship entitled her to be. Every night she would slip further and further down the rabbit's hole. Her body had betrayed her and she would never have the family she'd prayed for endlessly. She spiraled. She would be gone, out with a friend, had to go on an errand, but never came back with anything, or she simply needed some space.

Whenever she was around they argued about irrelevant things that spiked her attention. Nothing she could say or do made him tell her to leave.

He held on as long as he could, with the hope that she would realize what she could have, what they could have together. They could adopt and have a happy family. But Kari was oblivious. Kari would pack her things and leave for weeks at a time and then appear, eyes filled with shadows speaking of her needs and heartaches and smelling of regret and shame. Bucky realized that Kari had died when the baby had and that she was never coming back. He had rejected her many times upon that realization, but she would find a way back into his life high on whatever drugs she'd found. She would leave notes taped to his rearview mirror, steal his work clothes and hats, and draw butterflies on the windows with soap while he wasn't home. Bucky would eventually cave as if they were a luxury item on sale.

They would spend three days in the throes of passion filled with alcohol, cigarettes, and limited sunshine. When he felt like they would work out Bucky would see the signs. Sometimes it seemed like Kari's skin would start to visibly crawl after she had stayed with Bucky for a few days.

She would give the impression of being unnerved restless, and downright uncomfortable. Her conversation would die, her eyes wouldn't make contact with Bucky's, and she'd end up locking herself in the bathroom with a fifth of whiskey.

The tops she stayed with him were maybe a week's time and that was only because her ride had a flat or was held up by traffic or some other lame excuse they'd use not to pick that train wreck up. When she'd get the itch, she would begin a quarrel or throw something at the wall, and shortly after, flake off again.

The last time, Kari had flaked off for about two years and counting. Bucky hadn't heard nor seen the hide or hair of that girl. Still, Bucky could close his eyes and remember every curve of her beautiful body splayed in front of him, remember the taste of her warm sweet kiss, feel the warmth of her breath against his neck, and see the glint in her dark seductive eyes as they stared up at him with those pink pouty lips that had always tasted like strawberries and cream.

The boiled chicken has been loaded into the back of a sleek black cargo van. Not simply any cargo van, but one pneumatically engineered to provide the chicken with sealed in freshness until further forensic investigation could transpire. He needed Bus on the community center slash crime lab conversion duty pronto. Because of Bus's medical condition, some of the people didn't understand his cousin. They ridiculed him for his differences and never took him seriously.

Bus had been dubbed "Short Bus" in the micro town of Puckett where Bus was the only child to suffer from Down Syndrome. It didn't mean that Bus was stupid or ignorant, but that he handled things in his own manner.

His own way, "The Bus way".

Bus was Bucky's inspiration. He never let anyone stop him at anything he wanted to accomplish. He kept right on going and pushed through each day. Bus on the other hand was proud of his nuclear title. He would always retort to anyone who called him Short Bus with "I don't ride the short bus. I drive it and pick up all of you 'fuckers."

The Gulches' recreational area was trashed and the warm spray that lit onto the dump site made the papers and filth a pulpy massacre under the Sheriffs' shoes.

A crowd had gathered near the opening of the trailhead as Bucky pulled a candy bar wrapper off his sole and scraped off what was clearly not a peanut-infected chocolate bar. He saw the cause for commotion when he arrived as he brushed his shoes on the ground as he walked.

"Bucky! Over here, they found something." Bus's voice called him from amidst the mob.

In the purple-gloved hands of a perky yet somber female investigator were two evidence baggies, one with a black sock inside and another with several cigarette butts imprisoned inside the flimsy, two-walled, plastic container. The investigator brushed back the ebony flyaways at her temple as she handed off the evidence to her colleague.

"We haven't tested either item for chemicals or substances as of yet. We won't know for sure yet if these have anything to do with the vics, but if we come across anything interesting we'll be sure to give you a call first thing, Sheriff."

As the mob cleared away following up the evidence Forensic Investigator Fiona Peach had thrown to them she blew the steam off of her gas station cappuccino and leaned against the bumper of the SUV. Anyone who knew Fiona Peach personally was aware of the stern expression that would develop on her face when she focused on work or talked about a case. Her dark brows would scrunch up together and her jaw would clench as her blue diamond gaze took a needle and stitched all the pieces together before her.

Her fitted FIU "Forensic Investigators Unit" uniform was worn proudly, however Bucky could envision her off the clock and out of those khakis and in painted-on jeans and a tight white tank top down at Floyd's and shooting blue bombers with him into the wee hours of the morning. He enjoyed the way her mouth would form around each word and when she laughed her dark lashes would dance across her sun-kissed cheeks.

"We should be able to find out the ID of the intact body, but as for the skeleton, it may be a tougher stretch to figure it out. After about two to three weeks a body has already begun to decompose in water, and this is torrid water and temperatures which factored in and explains why the skeleton is without phalanges."

Investigator Peach reached into the pocket of her windbreaker with the emblem of FIU above her well-formed breast. She pulled out a tablet and tapped the screen several times as she opened a program and then swiped holding up a representation of the anterior portrait of the human skeletal system.

"You think we won't be able to find out the identity of the skeleton?"

Bucky stared at the tablet in the palm of her hand and affirmed that it was incredibly difficult to do with Peaches so close. He could faintly smell the fragrance of her shampoo and the detergent she used in her washing and an image of a golden queen bed at the Cowrock on an early Sunday morning came to mind.

"No, that's not what I'm saying, Buck. As you probably surmised on your own, the skeleton has probably been deceased for a while longer than the other, because the hands and feet usually fall off of a submerged corpse after it has decomposed in water. See, right here at the wrists and ankles there is a disconnect."

Fiona blew up the screen and zoomed in until Bucky could see similarities when she tapped on the screen and popped the appendages off, one by one, like Mr. Potato Head parts, and then dragged the feet and hands into a virtual jar of formaldehyde.

"I don't believe that they were forcefully removed. I didn't see any abrasions to the bones which flagged me that the soft tissues and ligaments had given way.

"What I'm saying is that we can't analyze the skeleton, because the hands and feet are missing. It's definitely going to cause us some hiccups along the way, but we've got dental records and we'll run various DNA analyses on both of them. I'd count us lucky that this isn't salt water. I don't put a lot of faith that we'll actually find some evidence that links to either of these victims in this nightmare, but the handkerchief and the cigarette butts look like fresh debris."

"You do that, Peaches, I'm on my way to Bear Den Creek. Let's head out. Bus, you've got some work to do in town."

Bus had not been happy to have Bucky follow him in the cart all the way back to town and then left behind to supervise the conversion of the community center. Once Bucky explained the importance of what the job entailed, Bus was eager to meet the meticulous needs of Puckett.

When Bucky drove away at the police station, Bus hopped into his squadcart and piddled down to the diner to visit with Maryanne.

Bear Den Creek had once been a Native American settlement before the Industrial Revolution, since then it has become the overflowing town for miners and drifters, now it was a peaceful settlement nestled into the mountain fifteen miles North of Puckett.

Bucky pulled his Dodge Charger towards the fluttering caution tape that encircled a bridge over Bear Creek and a grouping of trees. As he exited the truck, a big burly man in overalls lumbered towards him.

"Orson, I got your message and came over as soon as I could."

"Things flush downstream every day and especially during heavy rains like we've been havin', but nothing like this Bucky. Not a hand."

"Let's take a look at them and we'll decide where to go from there."

Chapter Four

Kat pulled the Jaguar onto the exit from Highway 348 that led into a dusty county road past a school, park, and many brightly themed buildings in bright autumn colors that dotted the minuscule mountain town. She was welcomed by a large wooden sign that read "Welcome to Puckett" in weathered paint.

At the corner of the narrow street was a gas station that squatted in the scenery like a big bullfrog. Her GPS had previously stated that Quickies was in the area close to her next house call. She'd fill up and then look around the town to locate the house, because as soon as the Jaguar's pristine front Pirelli tires met the gravel road her GPS and phone had lost signal.

As Kat drove down the street the Jaguar's engine growled. Her toe could barely touch the sensitive gas pedal and the sleek crimson car would jump forward as if impatient for an open stretch of road. Her eyes inspected the four-walled structure with large front glass windows. Quickies was a newer constructed building than any of the rest of the buildings, but just as run down. It had a set of gas pumps in front where she pulled up to an outer pump. The Jag's gaslight had come on somewhere between Blairsville and Owltown from the direction of her last house call.

As she pumped gas she gazed around the small parking lot. On the other side of Quickies, there was a second set of pumps for non-ethanol and diesel fuels. She could see the backside of a library on the next corner and a Post Office across the street. The GPS had shown that a Post Office would be next door to the Ballard home and across from a library. Not much was going on at this little hole-in-the-wall joint.

Quickies catered to truck drivers and patrons as they traveled along the Russell Scenic Highway and between surrounding towns. It was a convenience store that carried tobacco products, fuel, and everyday items sparsely stocked on their shelves. Puckett was small and not accommodating in the way of lodging big trucks and that cut down on trucker traffic even more, but they'd catch a straggler or two.

Adequate parking is key in most business establishments in modern society. In Puckett, it was like playing musical chairs without the chairs.

The gas nozzle clicked when her tank was full. She returned the nozzle to its holster at the pump and then walked inside to pay since the reader was Out of Order. Puckett seemed to be a Cash-Only town.

There wasn't much to the store itself as Kat scanned the room about the size of a pack of gum. Two shelves stood in the center of the building and a twenty-five-cent candy machine sat beside the front door and was the first thing seen upon entry.

Upon entering the store a raspy-voiced cashier greeted her in a sing-song voice as she checked out a customer in line. A man with a mustache who wore a trucker cap joked with the cashier about whatever they'd been speaking about prior to her arrival. Kat walked in as the cashier leaned forward on the counter and whispered to the man. Her eyes darted back and forth suspiciously.

"We are living in paradise, my friend."

The mustached man laughed and left out of the door. He stopped a man on his way in and pointed to the cashier who was shaking her fist at him.

She called out to anyone who listened, "Y'all better get Bucky down here before I jump over this counter."

The other men who stood in line or sat at nearby tables as they waited to buy their lunches or eat them there, laughed loudly and ribbed each other. The entertainment appeared to be welcomed by all and it felt routine to Kat as she stood awkwardly by and allowed the inside jokes to play out.

Kat felt like she was on a Mayberry Acid trip as she retreated to the back wall where the drink coolers were located. She walked right past the register and the half wall built that put a barrier between employee and customer.

A wooden fence to keep this cashier under control.

Kat chose a bottle of water and a bag of chips for later when she'd be on the road and snackish.

Kat took her goods rather cautiously to the rabid cashier who shouted at a bearded bald man in overalls and a flannel shirt that she was gonna open a can of whoop ass on him and anyone who stood aside from him. They all roared with laughter and it was Kat's turn as she placed her items on the counter. The brown-eyed cashier looked at her items and then at Kat as if viewing her from a great distance. Her eyes narrowed none too subtly.

"I also need three packs of Virginia Slims." Kat looked at the selections and hers wasn't in sight.

"You know not many people smoke these around here so I have to order them special and keep them aside for my reggies. My regulars come in and are so thankful because otherwise, they'd have to go to Helen. But I got you. The next truck is coming tomorrow morning." Ruby winked slid the three packs towards Kat and typed in her total on the computer screen of the cash register.

"$85.79. Cash or card, hun?"

"Cash." Kat handed $100 to the woman who seemed to be perplexed.

"You going to trust *Ruby* to give you the correct change back. Better check for wooden nickels."

"Al, you better watch yourself." The cashier called from over Kat's shoulder and flipped him a stout bird and the man chuckled as he threw his trash away and headed for the establishment's front door and stopped short.

He turned towards the cashier and waited for her to quit talking.

"It's Friday and the bank's closed, and Lisa hasn't brought me my change yet, that woman." She shook her dirty blonde head and gritted her teeth.

"Hey, Ruby, I heard your old boyfriend with the ponytail was coming by later. He's going to break that bathroom of yours in."

As soon as the moustached man in the trucker hat said ponytail Ruby's face lit up in the same shade as her name and Al dove out of the doors for cover as if she were a live grenade.

Ruby held up her hand to calm herself and closed her eyes as if she were searching for that inner peace and then regained her composure and smiled widely at Kat.

"You're new here, but that *shitter* has one thing comin' to him. He *ain't* my boyfriend. He comes in here and eats and eats and then shits in my freshly cleaned bathroom. I have to keep that up. But it keeps me humble."

She said as she lit a Marlboro 72 and puffed out smoke with each syllable.

When she finally handed Kat the change. Kat discreetly noted that it was correct as she dumped the change into the side pocket of her messenger bag. She nodded and then left the building before Ruby could strike up a conversation with her too. Kat had places to be and went back to the privacy of her car and removed a small day planner from her bag. She flipped through the months, found September, and then marked an X through the seventh.

Yesterday had been a day of driving and she still needed to find somewhere to stay on her off week. The dead cell reception meant now she couldn't search online for any short-term rental properties in the area and settled with mapping out her week instead. Her planner stated in a bright pink highlighter that her next patient was Dorris Ballard in Puckett, Georgia.

In her line of business as a Travel Nurse, Kat had been all over the US and now all across the Appalachian mountain ranges to see patients who lived in small towns that lacked proper hospitals or clinics that didn't carry or support their medications or treatment. Her job was to assess patients and pass the information along to their doctors. Kat cared for people with debilitating disabilities, terminal illnesses, and chronic pain patients, and reported all assessments back to their assigned doctors.

The major hospital she was contracted out of in Knoxville would pay Kathy a handsome stipend for travel expenses. She could book her own hotel, and pay for gas and food along the way as Kathy. Whatever was left was hers to do with as she pleased.

Sometimes she would receive emails or calls about the improvement in her patients' health and would receive many thanks for being there in their loved ones' last moments. She was good at what she did. She had the perks and ease of not having to stick to a 9-5 job each week, she could travel and see the world. The hourly pay wasn't half bad either and varied from State to State.

Occasionally clinics would reach out to Kat about the bulletins she'd posted on her webpage to teach first aid or health classes at learning centers. Other times she would host webinars through video calls on her laptop or phone. Many of those patients simply preferred a video call over an in-person visit and she was more than happy to accommodate them.

She'd stayed in a quaint rental she'd found online about twenty miles from Lovers Gulch. The woman who rented the cottage to Kat had even woken up early to make breakfast this morning when she roused. Scrambled eggs, apple-wood smoked bacon, toast, and a glass of freshly squeezed orange juice. Kat stuck a *thank-you* note with a magnet to the fridge before she headed out the rental's front door.

On a map, Puckett sat twenty miles west of Helen, Georgia situated in the Cowrock Ridge of the Blue Ridge Mountains. It shared similar qualities as the tourist vista with Bavarian-style homes and buildings. A collection of businesses were stuffed into the little pocket of the mountainside. Big brand stores hadn't reached this place. There weren't any gaudy billboards about liposuction or attorneys seeking to help the people get compensation.

But it was a ghost town. Kat had rolled her eyes at all the superstitious mountain people that she'd met who were seriously afraid of going out after dark. Scared of the witches and haints of the Appalachian Mountains.

The Ballard home was on Main Street beside the Post Office just as the GPS had instructed before it gave it up. She maneuvered the paved streets towards the house of Dorris Ballard, an 89-year-old woman who suffered from severe rheumatoid arthritis for years, and then she would be done with that and all she'd need to do was send the email.

The Jaguar's engine was a soft purr as it prowled around the empty streets and stretched its languished body into a parking space. A parking space whose lines had been meticulously lined and perfectly painted. Kat leaned over into the passenger seat and lowered her cat-eyed sunglasses to read a small sign at the front steps of the Bavarian-styled home which read *"Pharmacy Around Back Please Ring Bell"* with an arrow that pointed into the direction that the stepping stones led to around the backside of the home. Kat checked her phone to confirm the address was correct and then gathered her medical bag and then exited the Jaguar and approached the front door. No doorbell in sight, she knocked on the wood. She waited and then knocked once more. She took a moment to look around the area. The house was located along the main strip of town. It sat loosely sandwiched between a post office and a hardware store that had a few vehicles parked in their respective spaces and left to run while someone went inside to execute an errand. Across the street was a bakery, it was closed by lunchtime and on either side of it was a library and a tiny movie theater with only one showing, an action movie with a renowned male actor accomplishing impossible missions.

An old man answered the door. He was bald except for a few sparse white hairs at his crown and had a permanent hunch in his back from years of sitting and sorting pills into containers. He stared over his thick glasses with bleary eyes and up at Kat. His saggy jowls raised into a genuine smile when he spied the bag on her shoulder with her ID.

"You must be the nurse. Come in. Dorris is in the kitchen. We were sitting down for dinner. Come in. Come in." He stepped back and held the door open.

Dorris sat at the table in a kitchen that she had once spent much time cooking meals for her family and now her hands had betrayed her after all those years. Swollen, aching, twisted, and knotted knuckles that refused to work correctly. They burned relentlessly as if she'd shoved her hands in the fryer grease. Her knees, ankles, and toes cried protest whenever she stood and walked. Years spent standing on her feet feeding the town of Puckett, back in the good old days when things were in full swing and the diner would be packed.

Present-day Dorris Ballard was confined to a wheelchair as she was moved from room to room about her home by her husband. Kat sat in an ornate wooden chair across from Dick. He sat close by his wife's wheelchair where he could feed her in such a loving demeanor. He carefully scooped a spoonful of the hearty soup prepared by Flora at the diner and ate the contents of it. She chewed carefully and Dick gently held her twisted hand.

Kat noticed pain when she saw it. It was all in the body language and Dorris winced each time she chewed.

The inflammation had settled in her jaw and every time she would bite down on the soft stewed vegetables her complexion would turn sheet white. Dick rubbed Dorris's back gently and lifted a glass of water with a white bendy straw to his wife's lips. She struggled to swallow and got strangled in the water. Dick gently patted her back until she came around.

"We are so thankful that the hospital could offer to have you come up here. Traveling takes so much out of her these days."

Dorris nodded with genuine relief in her tired eyes and winced again.

With red-hot joints that ached relentlessly, sleep came in moments stolen in the night by exertion. Exhaustion crept through her muscles and would leave and slammed the door behind it with a piece of her sanity right in its fist.

Kat received these praises from her patients in similar circumstances as Dick and Dorris's. They were grateful for her care and the convenience that her care brought to them. They were also fortunate that their insurance covered the expenses at all with it being such a new program offered by the hospital.

Before this job opened up she had worked in the emergency room graveyard shift. Usually, nothing exciting occurred. But accidents still happened in the wee hours of the night. Things happened like not paying attention or falling asleep while driving or residential horrors like house fires, robberies, or heart attacks. No one actually wants to be in the emergency room except for the occasional head who wanders in with symptoms of drug withdrawal and is looking for a shot of the good stuff. Kat was never bothered by the chaos that sometimes filled the ER. Her father's drunken hellraising had always left an indenture in her psyche that needed to be filled with a little hellraising of her own, but she'd chosen to fill it through voyeuristic ways.

But one of those long, crazy nights she'd found the program brochure for a Travel Nurse position and a program to train individuals in one intensive year through the hospital. That year had happened in a frenzy fueled by coffee, energy drinks, intense clinicals, the stress of everyday life, and long nights in the ER tending to the maimed and miserable clientele.

Here Kat was as she sat at a table with a fruit bowl across from two achingly sweet souls. She filled out the forms on her tablet and slid it toward Dick to sign the care waiver and rate Kat's visit.

"You'd think since I own this pharmacy I'd be able to help my Dorris more, but truth be told this place has dried up and everyone just goes to Helen for their prescriptions. Cheaper there too or so I've been told. We are out of the way and out of mind. Odd times we live in." He shook his head in doubt.

"That's kind of like my old hometown." Kat made small talk while she filled out the remaining forms.

"We had a huge mall at one time and people from all over the state would shop there, but something happened. Local paper said the owner sold his stocks too soon and lost everything. Even the mall to the bank. A lot of people lost their jobs and people moved out."

The elderly couple exchanged forlorn glances and Dick shook his head in disbelief at the change that can happen overnight as he gently patted his wife's hand. Puckett, like Sugardale, was old news. Bought out by big business in other cities. Big Business and kudzu had a lot in common, appealing from afar but constricting and smothering everything around it.

"This town ain't much anymore, but Dorris and I just want to live out our lives here and be here for the boys as long as we can. Life's way too short."

Boys?

This couple was a little too long in the tooth to have young children. Her mind queried as the two hopeful elder turtle doves before her prattled on about their precious boys how they both worked in law enforcement and how proud they were of them. They even had big portraits of their pride and joys hanging in the living room which Kat was herded to before her departure. The cramped living room was filled with sumptuous furniture and antiques all moved there from the back bedroom when Dick had it converted into the pharmacy. Dick and Kat stopped in front of a wall.

On either side of a shelf along the wall hung two ornate pictures of a broad-shouldered Sheriff with a sad, but charming aloofness in his eyes and a stout doe-eyed deputy.

After she left Ballard's, Kat drove to the park and sat in the Jaguar as she worked on an email to send out to Angela the secretary of the hospital's Outpatient Program.

The park was merely a patch of dead grass thanks to the season change and sported a set of swings, a rusty wrought iron bench with rotted seating, and a lonesome merry-go-round that was also in ill repair. It leaned on its axis off balance and a shiver ran up her spine and she turned on the heated seats.

Once she found a signal she would send it out. The email consisted of Dorris Ballard's analysis and overall condition since her last in-person visit. Dorris's health had continued to deteriorate every day since her diagnosis. Sometimes patients couldn't handle the life-altering news. Dorris had developed depression soon after her diagnosis and it caused their health to plummet more quickly.

They all knew it to be true. The end was near for Dorris. Her doctor had recommended this outpatient care as a way to be home with her family and friends. The X-rays on file showed that Dorris had level four-stage lung cancer that had been overshadowed by the arthritis for years, until the MRI.

A spot on her lung at the last visit provided enough evidence to do a biopsy which came back positive. Terrible news for anyone to hear, read on paper, or have to inform someone of to say the least.

She wrapped up her work email and it was ready to send. That meant she was free for the next week until her next client and she'd have to wait for Angela to send her schedule out for the following week unless she had to go in before resubmittals could ensue.

What to do until then?

She pulled out a silver zippo that matched her tin case, lit a cigarette, and then puffed it pensively as she stared at the three-way intersection with a single blinking red light hanging in the center. No traffic aside from herself and the big truck headed out towards the highway. Kat put the car into gear and eased through the empty streets. She gawked at the beautiful mountainside and the town of Puckett as a whole. A once thriving town with amusement rides built into the rocks with old faded signs of height and age requirements. An old snow cone stand boasted of being made with freshly shaved ice and hand-made sweet syrups stood next to a rusted teacup ride overgrown with kudzu, the vine that ate the South.

A little motel sat back away from all the excitement of the rides, concession stands, dry rotted game booths. The Cowrocks' front front window had a small neon sign with "vacancy" that blinked repeatedly. The rates should be decent here she surmised even though her job compensated for housing in her travels.

Again she parked in an impeccably painted parking space at the Cowrock Motel. There were 10 Units spread on either side of the main office. Inside the motel office, it was quaintly furnished with vintage seating, and tables, and decorated with taxidermied animals from foxes to squirrels that were scattered all around and hanging from the walls.

Kat spied a bell sitting on the counter dinged it a few times and then waited until a Middle Eastern man approached with a jubilant expression when he saw Kat.

They probably didn't get many tenants in these motels now.

"Good afternoon, madam." He stood tall, chest open behind the counter with his hands clasped behind his back. He had a gold-plated name tag that read "Siley Saad".

"Do you have any vacant Units available for the week?" His ebony brows raised.

"One bed or two? Travelling alone? ID? No ID?" Mr. Saad raised his thick dark brows in question.

"One will be fine. Traveling for business and you can run it on this card."

Without listening to the motel rates, Kat handed Mr. Saad her driver's license and compensation card issued by the hospital to be paid through and to charge fuel, food, and housing. He checked her cards, copied her information in his log book, and then smiled.

"Wonderful. You can come see the rooms and choose for yourself. All vacant. All very clean. Breakfast included, but now offered at Floyd's down the street. Wonderful cooks."

He unhooked a wad of keys from underneath the counter and gestured to her to follow him.

Chapter Five

Bucky couldn't wrap his head around the events over the past twenty-four hours. A recent homicide and skeleton at Lovers Gulch and remains found in Bear Den Creek? He didn't want to beg the question, because in law enforcement things could always get worse.

He had called and checked in with Fiona's team first thing this morning and then dropped by the community center to see how far Bus had gotten with moving everything around to make room for the makeshift crime lab.

He had instructed Bus to push everything to the walls at the back of the room and box up anything loose. The Forensics team would be heading that way in an hour and Fiona would call him if anything turned up in the evidence discovery.

They had already identified the man as Aaron Michaels, male, thirty-two, five foot six, brown eyes, black hair, who had worked at Jerry

Jenral's for thirteen years after dropping out of college. He'd gotten a college scholarship in High School from playing Varsity football, but once his Senior year ended and he moved out of his hometown to seek his fame, his dreams veered away from a touchdown when academic life tackled him from all sides. He lost his scholarship, his comfy dorm room, and he'd lost his ambition for life and so for thirteen years he'd stocked items, scanned item after item, and locked up the store each night as manager and key holder.

What did Aaron Michael do to someone to have something so horrifying done to him? To be poached in a hot spring to the death was never on anyone's list of fears but to the surrounding community as the rumors slowly caught fire and fear began to brim in the eyes of all Puckett natives it was soon jotted down along with other local legends. Sure people go missing all the time on the Appalachian trails, but nothing ever like this.

People get mugged on highways and trails, and people get shot or maimed in domestic disputes, but this was cultish and disturbing even with Bucky's experience.

The town was sinking and the people had attempted to bail it out. The ones who chose to plug the holes went down like lead ships and the others bailed and left the others behind to seek brighter horizons. As far as Bucky and the rest of the town were concerned they would survive. Their town may not be what it once was, but at least it *was*.

He drove to Gillan's Produce, the grocery store at the backside of the Post Office and spoke with Lisa, the co-owner and wife to Ike Fleming. Ike had given her a list of items to have delivered to the community center for the Forensic team such as refreshments, snacks, and of course coffee. The Forensic team would be burning the midnight oil if Peaches had anything to do with it.

Bucky sat parked at the side in the pot hole riddled parking lot of Gillan's in his squad car, and his eyes bored holes in the walls of the community center when he looked away from his notes on this case. The graphic picture of the body at Lovers Gulch was displayed against the Manila folder. It wasn't really his jurisdiction anymore, but it was on his home turf and whoever did it had scared his people and that made it personal. Personal affairs did not mutate the law, but he had an inside operative that could let him in on the details.

He watched Bus studiously complete his assignment as Lisa Fleming pushed a buggy filled with the order down the street where Bus fully intercepted it. The Deputy quickly disappeared into the building.

In the dying evening light cast by the sunset, Lisa pushed the empty buggy back to the grocery store. She waved at Bucky and tootleooed as she disappeared indoors.

Bus promptly followed suit and continued his inside duties. As Bucky began to turn the key in the ignition he saw a flicker of gold from his left side peripheral.

Siley the motel owner walked alongside a young blonde woman dressed professionally in a white blouse, cream slacks, and a light navy jacket. They strolled from Unit to Unit and Siley unlocked each door to show Kat the amenities.

The motel concierge would soon be making a beeline to the grocery store to fill her hotel room's fridge since he stocked each unit as needed with the minimal traffic in the town. As they stepped into the last unit Bucky looked at her candy apple red drop top with Georgia plates and illegible numbers from the direction it was turned. It was lightly dusted in a fine layer of dirt from the unpaved county roads that her GPS had probably run her car down on a wild goose chase trying to locate Puckett. She would have had to zoom all the way in to see it on a map and most of the time it didn't register.

The blonde and Siley reappeared and she pointed at the last Unit they had viewed and nodded her head in approval. They disappeared into the Unit and Bucky waited a few minutes before he cranked up and watched the blonde return and walk to her vehicle. She removed a large suitcase from the trunk and then proceeded to roll it to her room in Unit 10. She locked the unit's door behind her and got into her car. As she backed out of the parking lot Bucky could clearly read a Fulton County number.

Siley's form exited the motel office and hurried over to Gillan's to get his new tenants amenities before she returned. The Dodges engine roared to life and the AC blew cold and then a continuous stream of warmth spread across his face. It should have comforted him in the chill Autumn nights that were blowing in, but it didn't.

Maybe it was the recent discoveries and the reporters calling his phone that had his stomach in a knot. Bucky's small speck on the world had gotten shaken up and it didn't settle well with him. This wasn't some junkie that broke into someone's home or an accident.

It *was* murder.

Aaron Michaels had been *brutally* murdered and a lot of preparation had gone into it. As for the hand in Bear Den Creek that was another case entirely and more than likely remains of an unfortunate loss along the Appalachian Trails. Bears and other wild animals could drag bones and all manner of things from one side of the mountain to the other. All of the evidence would continue to be analysed by Peaches and her crew.

Siley walked out of Gillian's with his hands filled with plastic grocery bags with a red *Thank You* on the sides and determination in his eyes as he made a beeline towards Unit 10 until Bucky rolled his window down and called out to him.

Siley turned on a dime and sidled up beside the black and white patrol car. "Sheriff Ballard, how good it is to speak with you today. How's your Aunt?" He shifted the bags into one hand and shook Bucky's hand in greeting through the window.

Everyone knew his Aunt's condition and how difficult it was for one of the two matriarchs who had lived in the time of Puckett in its prime to have to hang up her apron for the last time. People had once come from miles around to experience the fair town built into a mountain complete with the waterfall slide that was built under a natural waterfall that had become so clogged with debris it had dried up, teacup rides, panning for gold, several different fair games from horseshoes and of course the food provided by Floyd's.

In the 1950s Dorris Jean Wood started working at Floyd's Diner at the tender age of sixteen waiting tables. It was there that she met

Flora, the daughter of Floyd and Florence Peach. Florence had died giving birth to Flora in 1933, a year after the diner's first opening. He had been left to raise their daughter Johanna alone.

When Dorris met Flora they became fast friends in a world of men. Working men. Strong. Brilliant. Classy. Some, not so classy, not so strong, not so brilliant. They held fast together and worked their way to running the entire diner by 1959. Floyd had begun to tire more easily and couldn't stand up as long as he once was able and when the barstool next to the stove wasn't enough he stepped back and let the twin flames have their reign of fire.

By the mid-sixties, Puckett was an ant race of entertainers from around the states, consumers, performers, stage acts, men, women, children, exotic animals, and bizarre exhibits.

"Not the best. She's been home mostly and cooped up inside going stir crazy from not being able to get up and do like she wants to. It's been hard for her to accept."

"My sincerest apologies for Mrs. Ballard's health and to your Uncle and cousin. She is a special lady and a fierce cook. For me, she once cooked Mujaddara and Falafel just like Ommi used to make when I was young. The people of the community owe much to Mrs. Dorris and Mrs.

Flora." He said with genuine admiration as he shifted the plastic bags in his hands.

"I appreciate that Si. On what I called you over for, and I'll let you get back to what you were, but I see you got some business today."

Bucky nodded towards the Motel and Siley nodded in return with glee on his face.

"Yes. Very nice young lady in a bright red car. I cannot discuss my tenants' private details. Even with *you*. It is in poor taste for me as a host."

"I understand your priorities, I just thought I'd ask. We've got an investigation underway and the community center will be very busy and some may need a room. Might need to stock up more than one fridge. See you later."

Siley nodded, and seemed relieved to not have to divulge any private information about his once in a blue moon customer and thrilled at the possibility of more clientele to board in his vacant motel. He dipped his head quickly and turned to continue on his concierge duties with a little extra pep in his step. The entire property should be spotless as Siley was very particular and had lots of time to tend to every tiny detail.

Every surface was squeaky clean and every stone affixed in the dirt just so like a bird preparing his nest with twigs and pretty berries to attract a mate but in his case weary travelers and sightseers.

Bucky drove past the Little Red Schoolhouse as he followed the road that led out to the main Highway 348 that came out a few miles past the scenic Appalachian trail. He'd drive out towards Helen and then come back through after dark before heading back to Puckett.

He patrolled around these trailheads every night alone or with Bus and kept their eyes out for vandals, junkies, and to make sure that no one was out drinking and driving. These mountains had become a popular tourist spot in the early sixties and business had boomed and now in the larger cities like Puckett's adversary, Helen had absorbed all influx of tourists and trade.

Puckett caught the runoff from the city and it was enough to keep the town afloat. Stragglers and sight seekers wandered down through the wilderness and got their fill of nature to find Puckett hidden away in the palm of the Cowrock ridge.

The wide beams of Bucky's charger cast the asphalt in a washed out glare that hung shadows on the trees as the steel body rumbled down the stoic highway.

His Aunt crossed his mind, one of the two important people in his life who had always been there for him, and he could do nothing to help her.

She wasted away in pain and the depression ate away at her mind.

Try as he might, his Uncle could only do so much for her in his old age and still nothing would pull him away from his wife's side in her most dire moments when she needed him, even through the nights when she wailed for hours on end. It could become maddening for a caretaker so close and that's why Bucky had suggested Bus to come stay with him. Bus could take care of himself, but he still needed someone in his life to be there for him too and his Uncle had his hands full.

But what about Bucky?

He felt ashamed to even ask that question in the confidence of his own mind. *What about him?* He was Sheriff in a one horse town forgotten by the world. If he ran off the road and rolled down the mountain he'd be another report in the news of an unfortunate accident and only a handful would mourn him.

He couldn't think like that. He shoved those thoughts deep down into a hole in his mind and tried to think of other things. The murder was all his brain could dredge up to stave off the guilt of his selfish inquiries.

Aaron Michaels turned boiled chicken. Hands and feet bound or rather hogtied. Flesh and meat swollen with water, skin peeling away like a blanched tomato to expose soft meats underneath. His face and body beneath his clothing parboiled to the point of being unrecognizable enough to distinguish identity aside from dental records. Michaels hadn't been one to keep routine visits with his dentist, but Fiona Peach had a fine team working with her that managed to track down the dentistry office that had closed down years before but had kept all medical files in a You-Store-It in Blairsville, Georgia.

They worked fast as was Fiona Peach's forte and she'd honed that skill over the past ten years in her field and had formed her own forensic investigative team specializing in lost and missing persons and working with the Appalachian Rangers at times. An average of six people go missing on these trails every year and the occasional murder caused by stabbings, kidnappings, robberies on the lonesome trails, but nothing quite as gruesome as Aaron Michaels.

His headlights followed the winding road until they reflected off the taillights of a car ahead pulled off on the shoulder of the highway at the Hogpen Gap trailhead. The wide wooden fence alight in the moonlight was a barrier holding back the sea of stars in the sky. A full moon sat suspended in the black ocean and rained its radiance down upon the deciduous oaks that spread across the landscape below. Bucky could make out a silhouette as it stood at the trail marker as his squad car eased over onto the shoulder beside the candy apple red Jaguar. The silhouette turned and approached his vehicle slowly. Endless chatter from the radio spilled out of the dashboard of the car.

"Sorry to bother you just stopping to make sure everything's alright. Having car trouble?" Bucky called out of his window.

A deep soulful voice on the radio called out to Sugar on the line and received dead air, but the message was cut short as the woman bent over and hit the power. Dead silence and only Bucky's car's engine remained aside from the midnight calls of birds and yipping of wild dogs in the distance.

"I'm sorry I couldn't hear you over the radio. No, car trouble here. I'm taking in the scenery on this austere night and getting some cell service." She stood beside the car and held up her phone defensively.

Her gaze remained on the moon.

"Full moon tonight. Makes people crazy, I've heard." He chuckled and she looked at him intently.

"Not just any full moon, a Harvest Moon. I've always been a stargazer at heart." She giggled softly and even in the darkness Bucky could see the blush form on her cheeks.

"I guess I don't look up enough. But I should warn you if you aren't aware that people come up missing out here." Bucky pulled out a mag light and scanned around the area with the beam.

She laughed but cut herself short.

"Are you talking about Skinwalkers and Bigfoot?"

"Well, in a way I am, but you should be more careful. Meredith Emerson, sound familiar to you?"

"No, I don't know of Meredith Emerson." She crossed her arms defensively waiting for the reveal.

"She was twenty-four when she went on a hike about fourteen miles away from here on Blood Mountain. She was hiking with her dog and ran into another hiker, much older, he fell behind on the trail. On her way back down he attacked her with a knife and a baton."

"I can take care of myself," Kat interjected and pulled her cardigan around herself more against the crisp mountain air.

"Meredith had been trained in two types of martial arts and fought back, but he overwhelmed her. He kidnapped her and held her captive for three days before he killed her with a car jack. She thought she could take care of herself too."

"Did they ever find her murder?" She looked spooked by his story of murder and death.

"Yeah, he was the one who told her story, but I'm not speaking the name of a killer and giving his name life. He should have gotten the death sentence and especially after the discovery of three additional deaths."

She was quiet for a moment. Not sure what to say. "I'm certainly relieved that he's behind bars at the very least."

"At least."

"Well, I guess it would be in my best interest to get off these sketchy roads at night then, but I couldn't pass up this moon." And she turned and gestured to the moonlit landscape.

"It is beautiful, but even beautiful things can be deadly," Bucky assured her.

"Alrighty then I'm going to head on back, Officer. Thank you for stopping to check on me. Can't count on many people or do that nowadays."

"Sheriff Ballard out of Puckett and I never caught your name?"

"Kathy Walters, Atlanta. I'm actually staying at a motel in Puckett. The Cowrock?" She brushed loose hair behind her ear.

"I know it. Lived there my entire life. No wonder you couldn't get a signal. Iron Plate under the town screws up any cell reception. The only thing I can get out is a walkie signal." It hadn't been intentional, but Bucky felt like there might be something or could be something between him and Kathy. From the moment he saw her across the parking lot of Gillian's, he felt drawn to her. Even in his own mind, that sounded like creeper territory.

"Would you like to have breakfast with me in the morning? I know the Cowrock offers a complimentary breakfast at Floyd's."

Kat backed up from the window and bit her thumbnail looking a little distressed.

"Look, I don't want to put you on the spot or anything out here."

She waved away his words with her hands, "No, no, you are fine. I just have plans for tomorrow already and explained to Mr. Saad that I wouldn't need breakfast. I just... What about the next day? Lunch?"

"Sounds good to me. See you then. Goodnight."

"Goodnight, Sheriff." She waved to him as he pulled back onto the dark road and rolled away to continue his patrol.

After Kat made sure that the Sheriff's tail lights had disappeared around the bend she hurried and leaned over the door to turn the radio back on as the Love Doctor signed off for the night. No sultry message to Sugardale. Face clasped in her hands she screeched out a guttural roar from deep within her. She didn't have many things in her life that truly brought her peace and the moon. She wouldn't have known it was a Super Moon if the weatherman on the radio, Jet Tinny, hadn't mentioned it on the morning forecast.

Fuck the moon.

When she spoke to the Love Doctor his voice quieted all of the demons that clawed the inner sanctum of her brain. All the torment she'd lived through at school and the abuse from her peers, parental neglect from her father, and the absence of her mother, went away.

The only time Drunk Jim ever praised her was over the sheer fact she hadn't gotten knocked up yet and if she did he didn't want any part of it. The only reason he continued to do as much for her as he did was the life insurance check she received in her mother's death at sixteen. She was just a check to supply the beer in her father's fridge and to keep the power on so they stayed nice and cold. But once that ran out Kat kept the bills paid. Kat kept his fridge full of cans of piss water.

Kat kept the piss water nice and cold.

Tomorrow, Kat would be busy.

And the next day?

She'd go have lunch with that hobilly Sheriff at that diner everyone wouldn't shut about since she hit that county road off of the highway. She thought a quiet little hole-in-the-wall town like Puckett would provide more privacy than this.

Can't take a drive at night without someone showing up to poke around. Maybe that's why the town took a nosedive off the cliff.

Her mind raced as she felt caged in without an outlet. Maybe she'd made a mistake staying at that gaudy motel with the gold curtains and pressboard tables, but she'd put her entire housing expense on a week's stay. Sure, she could get a refund and leave, but now it would only render suspicion after this moonlit exchange.

She was stuck in Puckett like it or not and she'd make due. She had viable reasoning for her stay here on business, but picking up suddenly after booking for a week with the murder so recent on the news would throw up major red flags. Sheriff Woody was a problem and Sunday she'd find a way to get him out of her hair. She'd find out his patrol schedule at lunch. She'd butter him up good and then he'd let go of that information. He had ghosts in his eyes that yearned for companionship and she could use that to her advantage. She put her car in drive and turned around to head back to the pox hole in the mountain.

Chapter Six

Fiona Peach stared at the analytics screen and it glared back.

She sat in a metal fold-out chair that did nothing for the ache in her lower back. She removed her glasses and rubbed her eyes. Since Thursday night she'd been pouring over all of the evidence recovered from the crime scene at Lover's Gulch. But what *was* and what *wasn't* actual relative evidence had been the most difficult part aside from accessing the dental records of a retired dentist.

The entire scene of the crime was peppered with discarded to-go boxes and all manner of refuse from individuals who used the spot for a drop spot for drug-related activities or homeless squatters pitching tents and taking up residence.

The site had a bit of history wrapped in anguish and torment.

In 1838 a small detachment of escaped native Cherokee tribes were hunted and removed and sent forth to Chattanooga on the Trail of Tears. Among them was the tribe's chief's only living daughter, Tsula. After the band had escaped capture they fled to the safety of their sacred home in the Appalachian mountains with Tsula leading the way. Andrew Jackson's militia hunted them like wild game. Those who they couldn't capture alive, they killed. The bodies of the Cherokee were left to lay as the thousands of buffalo rot under the sun and their bones unburied and strewn across the land by wild animals.

Tsula had lost the majority of her tribe, her husband and father of their unborn child then, and her father, the Chief. The warriors were killed as examples in front of the women and children. Soldiers raped and murdered women and children and elders were left behind when they fell from exhaustion and exposure.

The location of Lover's Gulch and its name originated from what Tsula did once they reached the site of the waterfall. It was morning then and the sun rose and Tsula and her people gave praise to their Sun God and asked for blessings on her child, a boy that was born in chaos and taken by the elements. Tsula prayed that the God of Death avenge her tribe, her father, her husband, and their child as they moved on to the afterlife, spirits of the world.

"Blood of mine, blood of my people, blood of my ancestors, avenge them." Then as the legend went Tsula had sacrificed herself in the name of the God of Death. People said she hung herself from the cliffside, but others claimed she set herself ablaze and threw herself over the cliff and into the water below, and through the waters her blood still courses through the mountain.

Fiona shivered and shrugged on her windbreaker and sipped her lukewarm coffee. The numbers and letters on the screen blurred together, her eyes stung, and she needed a shower. She'd gotten as much as an hour of sleep after having fallen asleep in that metal chair. The golden bed at the Cowrock was calling her name. She just needed to fill out the rest of the form regarding the cigarette butts and handkerchief.

The socks that were recovered had been from Aaron Michales as he had been barefooted and the materials had dead skin cells from his feet. His shoes had been recovered from down below the lookout where Aaron had been pushed over, the abrasions on his chest and stomach and blood and tissue found on the rocks lip had said as much. He'd been dragged on his back as well and had abrasions on his upper back that told

Fiona that he'd been dragged by his legs. His right leg had been pulled right out of its socket whether before or after he had been hogtied with nylon rope. On his forehead, he had a large head wound and blunt force trauma and that hadn't killed him and it hadn't knocked him out either.

The analysis of the handkerchief and socks both had chemical substances on them which were Sodium hypochlorite solution and isopropyl alcohol. Bleach and rubbing alcohol. Homemade chloroform. Michaels had large quantities of the chemicals in his blood and lung tissues from the biopsy done on his lungs and chemical burns on his face. He'd been exposed to the chloroform in large doses. So the head wound could have been acquired when he inhaled the substance and went unconscious. He could have fallen and hit his head on something.

Fiona sighed as she typed in that the subject, Aaron Michaels, deceased, had died from *'asphyxial death'*. He simply had drowned.

It sounded much lighter than *'was brutally tortured and murdered by a sadistic pig'*.

She'd seen some stomach-churning situations in her time with the FIU. There were a lot of sick individuals out there, but there were a lot more good people too, and that's who Fiona worked for in all reality. The scared people who want to know what happened to their loved ones and who hurt them. That was Fiona's job, making sure the families of the victims had closure and that the perpetrators were brought to justice.

There hadn't been a case she had come across yet that she hadn't closed. She had a well-tuned team of like-minded individuals with a mastery of skills across the board and they worked well together. The other forensic bureaus called them the Scooby Gang even with their impressive turnover rates for open and shut cases. They didn't even have a fucking dog, but she guessed that was the whole joke. She was the bitch. They could snicker and talk all they wanted, but at the end of the day, Fiona knew she had put in her day's work and a day of goodness. She worked around so much death all of the time that she appreciated life much more. Life was a gift and some sadistic thief had stolen Aaron Michael's gift.

The metal legs screeched on the cement floor of the community center and echoed into its timbers and aluminum siding as Fiona pushed away from the endless logs of the deceased.

Aaron Michaels was a nobody working at a big box store. According to his credit reports he barely paid his rent and bills on time. The majority of his money was spent on pizza, takeout, porn, and online games. He didn't have an inner circle of friends and stayed out of touch with his family, except for his mom. She had been devastated and had kept saying if she'd just given him more money then he'd still be alive. Mrs. Michaels had been interviewed and thus interrogated about her deceased son and his habits and whether he had close friends or distant enemies. She couldn't offer any insight on why someone would do something so grotesque to her baby and what he could have possibly done to be subjected to such torture. She'd broken down under the weight, guilt, and accusations. As if having to identify her child's bloated corpse wasn't harsh enough for her reality and she had to relive it again answering the detective's questions. She just wanted answers and justice for her boy.

The final page of the report printed with the license and the last known picture of Aaron Michaels standing at a party holding up red solo cups in each hand and accompanied in the picture by two legible persons in the foreground. They were still unknown, but her team was on it and tracking down the suspect's identities and whereabouts for questioning. It was the weekend and a pain getting anyone to answer their phones.

It was almost 2 a.m. as Fiona left the community center and locked its doors behind her before she strode across the street towards the Cowrock motel. Her team had taken up the Units

1-5 as theirs at a nightly rate and Mr. Saad had been more than happy to accommodate them. The moon loomed above the sleepy town as Fiona's shoes crunched on the white gravel at the motel.

A black suburban was parked in front of Unit 5, Fiona's vehicle.

It helped to have another vehicle available to drive around instead of the big utility van they used at crime scenes that contained all of their equipment. A hefty van with a giant fingerprint on the doors attracted a lot of attention and that's not what they needed when running around towns they were stationed in, so they parked the van out of sight behind the community center and drove the Burb instead. Aside from the owner's modest Ford Crown Victoria like the majority of the old police cruisers used to be at one time, the motel's parking spaces were empty.

She was happy to help the businesses of Puckett and the people who had been so close to her grandmother's heart.

She'd spent her early childhood underneath her Grandmother Flora's and mother's feet at Floyd's diner, but Johanna Peach had other ideas. Fiona had spent other sequences in her life trailing her mother as she followed one man after another. Johanna would scream at Flora for yoking her with the weight of keeping and managing a diner for the rest of her life in a podunk town that had long since dried up. She'd berate her mother for hanging on to such a dream that wasn't even her own and she'd storm out dragging a young Fiona behind her and into the vehicle of some trucker she'd encountered.

Her mother had hungered for the unknown in a place like Puckett, where she suffocated under its overwhelming familiarity and redundancy day in and day out. She'd wanted more for herself, a more luxurious lifestyle than running a greasy spoon in the mountains.

After loads of therapy with a personal psychiatrist Fiona surmised that she could relate to her mother on an emotional level, However, in her adult years she still questioned her mother's motives her overbearing neglect, and the slew of men she had kept in tow. She'd used men and they had used her.

For a short time, she'd married a wealthy man with a taste for younger flesh. Fiona had been around eight at the time and many of her memories then had grown hazy after so long being repressed. She'd struggled with relationships herself and she blamed her mother because her father had never been in the picture and she wasn't even sure if her mother knew which one he had been.

Fiona had never seen what a healthy relationship consisted of just users and abusers. She remembered her grandmother retelling how her great-grandparents had met and how romantic her great-grandfather Floyd had been when he had proposed to her Florence. Fiona only wanted that unconditional love that they had in all the pictures scattered about and hung on the walls of the diner.

Fiona had never known her father, but even with her sets of skills and knowledge she still chose not to know him. He had never been a part of her life and her mother may have never told him, but it was a part of her that she had cut loose long ago.

She was responsible for her own future now and no one would have control over it again. Her mother included, as she was still hitting the boulevards searching for the next goldmine with orthopedic shoes to stagger into her life. Her mother had always taken care of herself and Fiona retained zero residual guilt to care for her maternal figure and instead applied that love toward her still-living grandmother.

If the diner needed help she would lend a hand. Taxes due? Fiona would take care of it. She'd done well for herself and stayed true to her own dreams while caring for the one woman in the world who had nurtured her even from afar.

When she turned sixteen she emancipated herself from her mother and went to live with Flora in Puckett. Since her cousin Maryanne had started working with Flora it had taken a lot of the work off of Fiona's shoulders. Especially when Dorris's health had begun to decline and she'd be out of town visiting doctors and specialists trying to pinpoint the cause of her failing health. They had been grateful for the slow traffic at the diner then, but it had spread another thick layer of stress on the already fragile family business. They'd made it work though as Dick tended to Dorris in their home, managed the pharmacy, and Flora with Maryanne's help tended to the diner.

As Fiona unlocked Unit 5 her shadow was cast against the door in front of her as the high beams of a car bounced around the side of the Little Red Schoolhouse down the street. Under the rows of dim street lights the bright candy apple red paint flashed like hazard lights.

Fiona stepped inside and peeped through the gold curtains as a long-bodied convertible with the top up rounded the corner, and pulled to a stop at the motel. When Fiona heard a car door slam she cracked her door and looked out past the motel's main office and towards the last Unit where the convertible was now parked.

A blonde female in a cardigan stepped around the vehicle and opened the trunk of the Jaguar. She removed several plastic bags before she shut it and went inside Unit 10.

Fiona shut the door quietly. Seemed like Siley was getting some business after all. Good news for Puckett. Maybe things were starting to turn up.

Fiona turned around and faced her Unit's room. A queen-sized bed, two nightstands, a chest of drawers with a small forty-nine inch LCD TV on top with cable, a small writing desk with a swivel chair tucked under it, and a small mini fridge sat in the corner and a microwave sat on top of it.

She'd have to ask Siley if he minded if she borrowed the swivel chair over at the Community Center if she promised she'd bring it back. He might allow it, but he was very particular about how he ran his motel.

She didn't travel with much, a couple of changes of clothes, a toiletry bag with makeup to hide dark circles after a long night of work, and her laptop The necessities. She pulled her blouse over her head and kicked out of her pants legs as she created a trail of clothes that led from the window to the bathroom.

The bathroom was standard with a toilet and a bathtub with a shower head and a burgundy curtain that popped against all of the gold and along the wall was an open floating countertop with a single sink.

She turned the shower on and as the steam filled the quarters she looked at her body in the mirror. Tan lines from working in the field under the sun clashed against the white flesh that infinitely stayed hidden beneath long sleeves and hours spent behind a computer screen in a chilled mortuary. Scars covered the curves and contours of Fiona Peach's body. Her unmanicured fingertips traced white lifted bumps left by cigarette burns and restraints and scars invisible to the naked eye. She turned from her reflection and stepped into the shower as it spouted from the head over her naked form. A sob escaped her throat as Fiona turned the knob until scalding water cascaded over her.

Chapter Seven

Kathleen Walker wasn't one to ask for attention. She was a wallflower and maybe she liked flashy cars, but she wasn't about to buy anything she'd need for Brad in Puckett. After meeting Sheriff Ballard Friday night she had decided to go back to Puckett and get an early start in the morning and make the most of the situation. She had several things on her list to pick up and some of the things that she'd need to take care of Brad once she found him.

Kat had decided to go to Helen because she didn't need any nosey something or other at the hardware store in Puckett to see her purchase anything. Everyone was so closely knit with the Sheriff in that town that if they saw something suspicious he'd be the first person they'd call. She'd have to be careful.

Kat was a fox in a hen house and the yard dog was sniffing around so she'd have to make sure the hens didn't make a sound. She could use this entire situation to her advantage and hide in plain sight here at the motel if she held her cards close enough to her chest. She had her job for cover. Sure, the hospital had Kat on an off week, but she was a freelancer too, and could find a quick alibi.

Relieved that she had finally gotten to hear the entire news report of some wigged-out couple that found Brad over at that dirty waterfall in Lover's Gulch and human remains that washed up in Bear Den Creek. She'd only caught the first portion of the report before the Sheriff had rolled up on her out of nowhere. Acquiring his patrol schedule would be vital to making sure everything went according to her planner. He'd already set her back and was causing her to feel rushed and it was taking the fun out of killing Brad.

However, Kat was one hundred percent positive that she'd never been to Bear Den Creek and definitely hadn't killed anyone there. This was her Circus, but that hadn't been one of her monkeys. Maybe it would help to throw off any possible suspicions as they dug up old skeletons in the Gulch.

To ensure that no one caught on to her facade Kat never bought her supplies at the same store and she always paid in cash if she couldn't she used one of the Visa Gift Cards she'd picked up around Christmas and would preload them when she got paid each week and included more if she received a bonus. More fun for later. More gifts for Brad.

She had spent the entire day Saturday viewing the sights that Helen had to offer and had driven fifteen minutes to Anna Ruby Falls to see if Brad was there. He hadn't been in the crowds of hikers and tourists that stood motionless as they posed for pictures and gazed at the beautiful Autumn foliage along the paved trail.

She then continued into Helen's boisterous atmosphere. What once began as a logging settlement in the late 60's was now a booming tourist trap and Kat had chosen the perfect time to hunt for Brad in one of the most anticipated celebrations of the year.

Oktoberfest had just begun and was in full swing and Kat discovered that Helen offered many choices of stores and at wide varieties and locations.

More Bavarian-styled homes.

More elegantly rustic architecture straight out of a fairytale, and herds of people that walked about the town and every twenty minutes a jaunty tune of *"Ein Prosit"* would commence and the rosy-cheeked celebrators would sing loudly along swaying to the meter and when the song ended they'd all raise their drinks and shout *"Oans, zwoa, drei, Gsuffa!" which meant "One, two, three, drink!"*.

In high spirits, they carried on scattered about and groups as they mingled in the traditions of Oktoberfest where the streets were exceedingly festive with banners, artisan crafts, and vendor stalls, and many people were in costume of Lederhosen and Dirndls, but some wore casual clothing or active wear for hiking. The aromas of roasted chestnuts, almonds, Bavarian pretzels, Spritzkuchen, smoked BBQ and soft earthy florals saturated the air in a delectable harmony while Polka music flowed from shops as did the endless fountains of beer poured into frosted mugs.

When her shopping was done in the late evening hours and after she had taken all of the goodies she would use to spoil Brad from the Alpine shops and out to her car, Kat claimed the bench in Helen Square as her stake out. She gathered her bearings as the busy-spirited gobs of bodies that ambled around in front of her. She sat on a bench set into the crook of a cobblestone wall and out of the way, while she scrolled on her phone at cars and her next housing option online.

The outfit she'd chosen was a beautiful black velvet dirndl with a red apron and a puffy-sleeved blouse underneath that had a generous neckline with red stitching that exposed the peach-toned flesh of her breasts. The bodice accentuated the curve of her ribs and breasts as her perky nipples peeped beneath the cotton fabric. The skirt was the shortest she could find at twenty-five inches and fanned out at her thighs. Add a pair of knee-high white socks, a set of black flats, and braided blonde pigtails with tiny black ribbons tied at the ends, she was indeed a sight for sore eyes.

She'd always been referred to as a *butterface* in High School meaning everything *but her face* was attractive. Since leaving that cesspool that was Sugardale she'd taken good care of herself and had her teeth straightened from the crooked booby trap it was then and all while working in the ER once it had been covered by her insurance after a year and she'd spent many hours watching "GRWM Get Ready with Me" videos online on to know how to properly catfish someone. Even she had to admit she looked pretty hot in the floor-length ornately framed mirror in the Bavarian shop. She blended in well with the crowds and she'd turned an eye or two but otherwise strolled about unnoticed as she stopped at stalls with handmade crafts, clothing, pastries, and Helen memorabilia out the wazoo.

Kat's viridescent gaze observed the bustling scenery from over the top of her phone in Helen Square. The streetlights had come on along with all of the Oktoberfest decor that bedecked the streets throughout Helen and absorbed the smiling jubilantly flushed faces of children as they ate ice cream in waffle cones at an umbrella'd table in front of an old-fashioned Bavarian Creamery. Fifteen feet away a young couple in the throes of love took engagement pictures with a photographer poised to take just the right shot with them, the Bavarian architecture, and the mountains cascading behind them. If a mad scientist could bottle up the energy that exuded from this city they could use it to power the world and go to the moon a million times over.

So much life was here in front of her and her voyeuristic heart pounded intensely when a man dressed in traditional Lederhosen and possibly in his late twenties or early thirties sauntered up to Kat as she sat seemingly engaged in her phone on the bench while she sipped on a Shirley Temple.

Without introducing himself the moustached man plopped down beside her and radiated a deep barley briny musk that seeped around her and made her eyes water. He took one of her blonde braids in his fingers and pulled it to his nose and inhaled as he tugged at it. He smoothed his thick mustache as his eyes scanned her attire. His eyes raked over her breasts and wandered down to the waistline of the short-skirted Dirndl and finally to the pink bow tied to her left side. Pink symbolized at Oktoberfest that she was single and ready to mingle.

A bow on the right meant married and a bow at the back was reserved for widows, waitresses, and children. Almost a cultural upside-down pineapple or loofah on a car antenna.

"What brings you to Helen, business or pleasure?" He leaned in closer and the odor of beer and bratwurst hung heavy on his breath. His arm stretched around the back of the bench and behind Kat's bare shoulders. In his other hand, he held a glass mug half filled with warm beer. He gulped the brew and belched as his fingers drummed on the wood until Kat lowered her phone and looked directly at him which made his stained smile grow wider like that of a Cheshire Cat's.

Out of all of the aromas that wafted around the air, the stench of beer hung acrid in her nostrils and dredged up a flood of unwanted memories from her childhood home. Drunk Jim as he staggered around cursing and throwing things in the kitchen and then Brad threw her down onto the dirty floor, not two feet from him he shoved a dirty rag over her mouth right as she breathed in to let out a scream.

Everything had faded to black after that until she woke up. Kat had woken with her head throbbing and woozy. Her lungs had ached and her brain became hazy and then the feeling of a scraped knee on concrete had spread like a web of fire across her shoulder blades.

Brad had dragged her across the floor to the back into her bedroom and laid her on her bed, a mattress on the floor. But then Brad was nowhere in sight and her clothes lay crumpled on the floor where he left them after he had ripped them off her unconscious body. Just as it had truly dawned on her what had happened Drunk Jim had stumbled down the hallway and stood on the threshold of the door, his hands braced himself as his eyes had narrowed at Kat's vulnerable and naked form that sat trembling on the filthy mattress.

Darkness shrouded his face as his lips curled back he gritted his yellow teeth at her and a foam dribbled down his chin. His hands had fumbled at the buckle as he cast curses in her direction. She had tried to cover herself and had begged him not to beat her, but her pleas were futile as he had struck her over and over with the belt with no rhyme or reason. There had been no talking to Drunk Jim.

He chose not to listen.

After that night Kat stayed home from school for almost a week. The school never even tried to contact her father and a truancy officer was never sent to make a house call for a wellness check on Kat's behalf simply because no one wanted to deal with Drunk Jim. He was known to get aggressive with visitors.

The first day back at school had been the worst part. The rumor was that Kat and Brad had hooked up in front of the Dry Cleaners where they usually only made out. Kat had begged for it and Brad had felt so spurned by Sidnie cheating on him with the line back from their rival team that he needed to get his worm wet and Kat had been more than willing. As soon as Kat had made it back to school and had stepped into the cafeteria at lunchtime between classes Sidnie had confronted her in front of the entire grade and said as loudly as was possible that Brad had come crawling back to her and told her that Kat was a dead lay. Her peers had erupted into laughter and whispered between each other as Kat had burst into tears and fled from the cafeteria.

Business or pleasure?

Kat didn't have to put much thought into his question. She knew without a shadow of a doubt why she was in Helen and it wasn't for business. Kat stowed her phone away in her bag.

"Pleasure." She replied, as she took a sip of her non-alcoholic drink and the stranger grinned with lust in his eyes. His moustache curled under his glazed eyes, she pulled out a fancy-looking metal case with ten Virginia Slims lined perfectly inside. She removed one and put the filtered end to her lips.

The stranger's eyes bounced from Kat's thighs, to her breasts, and back to the cigarette in her mouth as he wiped spittle from his chin.

"Can I bum one?"

Kat grinned her own Cheshire grin as she removed a second cigarette from the case and placed it between his lips. She removed a zippo from her bag, struck the flint wheel with her thumb, and the wick erupted into a solitary flame, an eternal flame, that she lit her own Virginia Slim. As she puffed out a smoke ring she lit Brad's.

Kat invited Brad back to her motel room and he was more than willing to join her. She'd told him the motel was in a small town about twenty minutes drive away. Brad blindly followed her to the parking lot. He wasn't a big talker, but he became quite handsy the moment they got in the Jaguar.

He had shoved his hands down her blouse to fondle her breasts that she'd teased him within the square and soon fished down the front of her panties as if looking for lost keys in a couch cushion. He grabbed her by the pigtails and his tongue seized her tonsils. Kat allowed him to grope and molest her until she finally pushed the man back to the passenger seat with a seductive smile and wagged her finger at him.

He sat back on the seat perturbed to be told to stop but given enough to entice him to follow through. She needed him out of the city, away from prying eyes. Oktoberfest celebrations would keep most in the vicinity distracted, but Kat needed to move. She had quite the surprise for Brad planned and he was going to die when he saw it.

Eight minutes into the drive Brad began to complain. He sat in the passenger seat rubbing his penis through his Lederhosen as he stared holes into Kat's form. She drove them through the winding roads of the mountain Northwest of Helen. He was ready to devour her. Kat blew him a kiss and then turned up the music on 105.3 strands of hair flying and framed around her face, freed from their restraints as she wailed out "You Oughta Know!"

Halfway up the Unicoi Turnpike Kat turned the radio down and faced Brad with a pouty face as she moved to the shoulder of the road. It was pitch dark except for the headlights and turn signals that flashed.

"What is it?" He asked with every ounce of annoyance one could muster. She'd dragged him away from the party to the middle of nowhere and had teased him to the point of frustration and he had begun to sober up.

"I think I heard the car make a weird noise. Can you go look?" Kat wrung her hands and fidgeted with her pigtails.

Brad looked quite perplexed and his eyes darted to the window and into the darkness beyond and back to Kat's arched back and the pink rosebuds beneath her white cotton blouse strained against the fabric.

"I didn't hear anything. How the hell could you hear anything over that."

He gestured to the radio. He was perspiring either from the high amount of alcohol he'd begun sweating out through his pores or from fear of what the Appalachian trail could hold. Brad was very superstitious. Before any game, he'd always wear the same socks. They were his lucky socks that he never washed for fear the luck would wash out and he'd lose the game. His silly superstition had led to an unhealthy case of athlete's foot.

"Please. Would you? I'm scared. There are Wendigos, Bigfeet, and- please, can you?"

She was now on the verge of real tears. A skill she'd learned in school with her teachers and when she would get sent to the office to speak with the Principal. He'd been a creep too. She'd always cry loudly and someone would rush in to see what was wrong and ruin any plans of his. Worked like a charm. Brad was no different. It seemed when women cried it made men uncomfortable and sometimes it made them horny, but usually their White Knight Syndrome would kick in and they'd have to save the day or they'd turn tail and flee.

In Brad's case, he was up Shit Creek without a paddle. He could take out and walk back to Helen on foot and brace the elements of the Appalachian trail or check the car out quickly and see what this seductress was going to do to him in that motel.

With much reluctance, he buckled.

"Fine. I'll go. Do you have a flashlight at least?"

Brad wiped perspiration from his face and regretted leaving his phone in his truck before Oktoberfest started so he wouldn't lose it or drop it. He'd planned on drinking until his Lederhosen fell off.

Kat smiled and nodded and dug through her purse until she held up a keychain flashlight that she'd picked up at a souvenir stand in the Alpine

Village. Brad was not ecstatic about walking out into the spooky mountainside and a stench emanated from him that only a predator such as Kat could sense immediately.

What Kat presented to him was faux fear visible to his eyes by her body movements and her facial expressions and what she represented for him was a frightened fuck doll. But what Brad embodied and produced now was cowardice and it oozed from each of his pores and onto her tooled leather seats.

He snatched the flashlight from her hand and threw open her car door cursing as he exited and then turned the light on. The tiny beam of light bounced down the road and in the trees and at the car and as he looked under it and on all sides confused. He poked his head back through the passenger door at Kat. He couldn't see shit with this light.

"I don't know what you are talking about. Did you run over something?"

Kat's frown was exaggerated by the Jaguar's interior light and her hysterical sniffling amplified by the turn signals momentary illumination.

"I don't know, Brad. It sounded like a back wheel maybe. I think I have a spare. Can you check?" She tossed him a puffball keychain with a single key designed for her trunk. It fell and he dove to catch it and bumped his head on the door.

"Be careful."

"My name's not Brad, it's Josef." He growled and reluctantly continued his inspection of her car and then stomped to the trunk with a keychain light in hand and unlocked it. The trunk opened and bounced against the hinges as he felt around in the trunk. Despite the keychain light he felt blindly around as he searched for a felt flap or hidden compartment for the spare, but felt slick plastic beneath his fumbling fingers. Under the hazy glow of the souvenir light, he saw the trunk was lined with some type of black plastic sheet.

"What the fuck?"

"Did you find it?" Kat had appeared suddenly and Brad turned around as she covered his face in a cloth soaked in chloroform. He grabbed her arms and at her throat as he struggled, but the chemicals had begun to take effect as his vision fogged and his muscles grew lethargic.

Kat pushed his chest and his five foot seven frame crashed towards the open trunk and his legs crumpled at contact with the bumper. Brad moaned as his body was half in and half out of the trunk's yawning mouth and then he was silent.

Kat loaded the rest of his body into the trunk with more effort than she liked. Brad had packed on some weight. She tied his ankles to his wrists and then fixed an automatic freshener with a motion detector to the corner of the trunk. She positioned it to spray directly into Brad's face. If he woke up and moved around a lot in the trunk the freshener would sense his motion and spray chloroform into his face. Kat replaced the canister of fragrance with a spray bottle filled with her homemade concoction and swapped the spray nozzles from the original canister onto the container of chloroform.

The idea had come to her when she was having a meeting with her supervisor. Kat suspected her supervisor had kept the freshener on the desk and pointed towards the chair to freshen the area as her clients or underlings would sit and then depart. But it didn't work like it should in practice. It would spit out sweet florals and momentarily distract her from the discussion. Then a thought had arisen.

What if it were chloroform instead of fragrance?

She would have crumpled in the leather armchair and taken a lengthy power nap.

It had come in handy a time or so and with little issue, but it had taken several attempts to work out the correct ratios. The concoction was stout enough to knock Brad out every time and for long durations up to three hours although she tried not to keep him locked in her trunk for more than a day. Too much and the chloroform would kill him and that was never fun, but she had accidents now and again. She'd finally found a happy medium that served its purpose well.

She could keep him in her trunk overnight, go back to the motel, and sleep like a baby knowing he was so close and would be ecstatic to see her face the next day. She still had to meet with the Sheriff at lunch, figure out what his patrol schedule was, and then she'd know exactly when she could spoil Brad. He'd have to just be patient.

Chapter Eight

Early the next morning, she got dressed and ready for her lunch date and went for a ride to collect her thoughts and air out the trunk some. Adrenaline in her veins pumped from the pure excitement and exhilaration of spending so much time with Brad and no one was the wiser. He hadn't made much ruckus in the trunk and hadn't drawn any attention to his whereabouts, but she would have to take the trash out eventually before anyone started to look for him.

Sometimes finding Brad was too easy. He was always in a crowd skulking around as he waited for a meek little lamb to sink his teeth into and Kat had once been like that naive little lamb. She'd been dealt a shitty hand and anteed up her innocence early. Kat had maneuvered around life seeing through a foamy lens of lies, neglect, abuse, and damned by her existence. Not everyone shared her childhood experiences.

Bruised fruit like hers became rotten after a time of being passed over and ignored. Experiences of that nature have a warped effect on a person's psyche and sometimes it creates a void. An immense pit that if left abandoned too long would either rot or sprout. Death or Life. Two choices. She could curl up and die from the weight of the events of her past or grow and become larger than life itself. Make the Brads of the world feel what she had felt.

Kat's pit inside of her pleaded to find Brad.

Find Brad. Remove his essence from this earth.

Well, she'd found him in the Gingerbread Town this time and quicker than expected, but still not a lost cause. If the Sheriff wasn't patrolling tonight then she could go through and take care of Brad. She bit her lip in frustration at the thought as she drove the Jaguar back down the winding dusty county road towards Puckett.

No, new updates today. No good music on. She just drove and listened to the symphony her tires made on the road and the wind that whistled through her loose blonde locks. Gospel would play for most of the day on Sundays and it wasn't her cup of tea.

Kat had never gone to church. But the church had come to her house repeatedly as a child. Not always the same people as if they'd take turns visiting the alcoholic Jimmy Walter's home like a petting zoo. Sometimes they'd bring along their children if they knew Drunk Jim wasn't home.

Kat enjoyed playing with the children but realized later on in life why they had brought them along. She was sure they'd tell their children after they left that if they drank alcohol, had premarital sex, or sinned they'd live like that and then they'd go straight to Hell. Kat and her rancid home became the town's example of how to fuck up your life.

They'd knock on the door and practically invite themselves inside to witness the squalor of Kat and Drunk Jim's home.

Their eyes had taken in the unswept and sticky linoleum floors. The weight of cobwebs and mounds of dust on the ceiling fan blades pulled them down to resemble some sad inverted flower. Trash bags of beer cans and bottles lay on the floor and any flat surface and littered the floor around the overflowing trash can in the kitchen. Their eyes had dined on the holes that dotted the drywall like pimples and the overturned and broken furniture of the Raging Room that Kat had personally deemed the Living Room.

The couch had been from the seventies, a groovy orange covered in various stains and frayed at the armrests and corners of its cushions. It had once seen better days.

The church people perched on the edge of the couch cushion and seemed visibly uncomfortable in the environment with astonished expressions as they attempted to lead a little lamb to salvation. Sometimes they would bring cookies, sodas, chips, and candies for Kat and she would scarf them all down before they left her sight. They usually only visited when Drunk Jim wasn't home and off doing whatever he did then. She didn't know. He'd never included her in his event planning. The church people continued to drop by on Sunday afternoons after the Pastors had fired them up to go out and find the lost lambs and speak to them in the name of Jesus and be saved. *Amen.* They spoke of Jesus, heaven, hell, fire and brimstone, and ashes to ashes and dust to dust. They shared the Gospel and then drove away in their BMW and rode that spiritual high of feeling right with the Lord to their beautiful homes with manicured lawns and overabundance of food. Whatever helped them sleep at night.

Puckett was in its state of perpetual desolation like a rotted shadowed version of its competitor twenty miles away. Buildings in the hues of Autumn foliage had chipped paint flaked off like leaded snow around the sides. More shops were empty and left abandoned in Puckett than there were ones that barely thrived off of their local regulars and occasional stragglers. Experiencing Helen first hand she could see how dead the fair town was now.

How had this town not turned belly up? Or was it currently floating topside down? It was definitely in distress.

The first sight someone would see of Puckett upon driving down the county road would be all of the fair rides underneath the cloak of the mountain that sat rusted, motionless, and unused for years. Nature had claimed the majority of the rides and stands in fingers of ivy that climbed through every mechanical niche it could anchor itself to and added to the dystopian settlements ever oozing charm. Amidst the ivy and weeds a Ferris wheel, that violated every safety code in the Carney history books of equipment violations, stood erect with empty seat buckets levitated and poised in an eternal tribute to the sun that beamed over its rusted integrity.

A large painted sign read 'The Little Red Schoolhouse' at the end of a large gravel parking lot. The school was also the smallest one she'd ever seen in person.

It probably had twenty students that attended from around the community. The building itself was a simplistic structure built from wood and painted barn red.

The school was out of session for the weekend, but a green Honda Accord and a white Kia Optima both in desperate need of a washing were parked at the front doors of the otherwise empty academic building.

Floyd's parking spaces were almost all taken aside from a space by the Sheriff's patrol car. The Jaguar rolled into the space and Kat sighed as she checked her reflection in her rearview mirror. She made sure her makeup was just so and had sprayed Chanel No. 5 on her wrists. She wore a deep-necked light grey cashmere sweater to fight the chill and paired it with a tight black leather skirt that ended just above her knees and her mid-thigh chunky heeled boots that stopped about five inches below the hemline. She was quite fetching. A bit of city flair in this overalls and suspendered town.

Before she cut the engine off Kat looked through the large glass windows of the diner. The barstools were all filled with several men hunched over eating their lunches and shooting the bull like they probably did every day at this particular time.

Locals.

The mustache man in the same trucker hat from Quickies sat next to an old black man with a large wooden stick propped up on the counter by his side. Four men sat at tables and enjoyed whatever they dined on as they carried on animatedly with each other and a waitress in a powder blue uniform and white apron while she made her rounds. The Sheriff wasn't among them but sat at a corner table where he faced the front doors and with his back to the wall. He'd more than likely seen her arrive as she glanced out the windshield.

The cowbell on the door rattled when Kat entered the diner and a few heads turned and gawked at her and an elbow ribbed someone in a joking manner.

Styrofoam carryout containers were stacked to the ceiling against the wall behind the bar. Three people were working in the kitchen. Two were prepping orders and their hands were a blur of meat, cheese, lettuce, and buns as they handled their short orders for the scant crowd and fished out French fries from the vats of bubbling oil.

Kat spied a spry little old lady at the back of the kitchen that stood before a giant griddle as she flipped burgers. She took a moment and breathed in the aromas of lunch prepared by the ladies in the kitchen. They worked in a little square maze with a steel island at the center.

The elderly woman stood in the back of the kitchen in front of a gas griddle as she walked close enough for Kat to read that her name tag said "Flora".

Flora flipped the meat patties over and the griddle sizzled in response. She wiped the sweat from her brow as she placed the bag tie on the wire rack that held all the buns and bread for the kitchen. The thin piece of plastic was just one among thousands that had been collected there since she'd first opened the diner with Dorris. It was a physical testament to how much business had come through their doors.

"Sadie, can you see what this lady needs?" She waved at Kat and then took a sip from her white foam cup and then went back to preparing her food.

Kat paused at the counter window and studied the menu. A petite black girl popped into view with a pad and pen, she scribbled at the top of the paper, shook the pen, and scribbled again leaving a mark.

A bubbly brunette walked to the counter in front of the domed display and chatted about all the delicious food on the line as she named off the buffet selections, rearranged the fried chicken, and stirred the contents of the giant pans. Fried pork chops and chicken tenders, green beans, cream corn, breaded okra, and for dessert was a red velvet sheet cake divided into eighteen uneven squares.

"Yes, ma'am, you can call me Sunny. That's what everyone says around here because I smile all of the time. Maryanne will come to your table. You can sit wherever you want, hon."

Kat dodged the empty tables that stood between her and the Sheriff. He stood up when she arrived and pulled her chair out. Kat looked at him quizzically but sat down nonetheless as he scooted her seat forward and then took his seat across from her and removed his hat.

Great, Prince Charming in the flesh.

She poured herself onto the cracked, blue leather seat and the taut fabric pinched and scratched at the threading of her pants. The top of the table had been lacquered and amidst the hardened clear varnish were bottle caps, postcards from distant family, and black and white pictures of a happy family in front of the store on opening day many years ago.

He smiled and nodded towards the menu when a waitress named Maryanne approached with a pad and pen and a warm friendly nature.

"Can I get you anything to drink or eat, ma'am?" She asked as she took an empty coffee cup from in front of the Sheriff. He must have already been here since this morning.

As the waitress recited the specials to Kat she felt that she wasn't all that hungry still. She'd had a big breakfast in Helen that morning as she'd collected all the necessities she'd planned for her and Brad's picnic. She'd bought a Honey Baked Ham and a string of smoked bauernwurst from a German smokehouse, a classic checkered picnic blanket, and a wicker basket. Other delectable sweets and powdered pastries she gathered were hauled to her Jaguar's backseat where she'd quickly gone to unpack all the food and placed them into disposable dishes inside the basket. Afterwards, Kat had thrown all of the store packaging and receipts away at a gas station and topped her tank off before hightailing it back to Puckett.

It had been a productive morning.

"Coffee, please," Kat answered to a hovering Maryanne who smiled and then took The Sheriff's order. Maybe she should have gotten something other than a coffee when she looked at the Sheriff's perplexed expression at her meager lunch.

"I'm sorry. I had a late breakfast. I should have waited."

The Sheriff shook his head dismissively.

"Don't worry about it. Kathy, right? It was late and I apologize for interrupting your stargazing."

Kat glanced down at her phone on the table Half past the hour and no cell reception.

Was the time here even accurate?

She was skeptical of the entire town and frustrated with the shoddy cell reception. She would have to find somewhere to pick up some bars again later tonight.

Maryanne returned with a tray and a coffee carafe filled with the dark bean brew. She removed a white ceramic mug, a matching bowl of white cane sugar, and a creamer vessel from the tray and placed it before Kat.

Kat thanked her and turned back to the Sheriff.

"You got it. Kathy with a *K* and no worries. You were doing your job."

Kat smiled warmly while she spooned in a spoonful of sugar and then stirred in her creamer from the tiny ceramic pitcher.

"That short for something?" He asked with genuine interest. She took a second to look at the Sheriff. He was tall, and his ears stuck out from under his mahogany hair that he probably intentionally kept longer because he thought it would hide them.

"Katherine." She blew across the surface of the hot brew and looked at the Sheriff. "So what about you? Bucky short for something?" She took a slow sip.

He chuckled "No, just Bucky. Why? What did you think it was? Buford or somethin'?"

Maryanne delivered his plate, an omelet, sausage, and bacon.

"I figured there couldn't be two Sheriff's named Buford. I don't know... Barnaby?" She sipped her coffee. The Sheriff dug into his omelette and chuckled talking about his name and his cousin's name. *His* last name.

The chair she sat in had a slightly irritating wobble and the cowbell rattled as the men at the bar got up from their perches and went wherever they went when not observed.

So much activity in such a small vicinity.

Stay on track. Less about you, more about him. She hated keeping up with the boring details of her fake life.

Get his patrol schedule.

"So what brings you to Puckett? There's not much around here any more to keep any one person's fancy for long, but the people are friendly and the food is good." He lifted a strip of bacon to his mouth and crunched it as he waited attentively.

"Oh. I thought you'd already come to the assumption of who I am, Sheriff. I understand you have been dealing with a full plate and I am not sure if I would be incriminating myself by telling you my business."

Bucky stopped still and stared at her his gaze narrowed across his plate at her, his demeanor had swiftly stiffened and his food was left untouched.

The yard dog sniffed around the hen house and the fox was dressed in chicken's clothing.

"How do you mean incriminating yourself?" Kat sipped her coffee pensively.

"It's a matter of doctor-patient confidentiality and I being the middleman of sorts can't divulge any of your Aunt's medical information. Just know that she is in good hands."

Bucky took a bite of his sausage and his entire body relaxed.

"You seem like a nice Sheriff and all, but if they haven't told you themselves then it's not my place ethically and legally."

He had a puzzled look that slipped into one of gloom that filled his face with shadows. Kat didn't know the reason why, but it seemed like he was overwhelmed and out of the loop. A good reason not to have to share on her part and maybe this moment was an up for Kat.

Two brownie points for me. More chit chat and then I'll slide a question in that pertains to when he'll be off next.

But he should be the one to ask.

After all, she didn't want to seem desperate.

"But since you asked I visited your Aunt Dorris with an outpatient program. I'm a travel nurse. I assess patients who are in remote locations and have debilitating illnesses that prevent them from traveling to seek care. I found this town charming and was informed by your Uncle about the Cowrock. He was concerned that I needed to rest. They are such kind souls."

Maryanne wove through the tables and chairs to top off Kat's coffee and to take the Sheriff's plate like a hummingbird collecting nectar from the throat of a flower.

"I appreciate the work you do, Kathy. It's needed in this world. We need more people who care. Not to just simply care for them, but to care *about* them."

Kat agreed with him while she stirred in more cream and sugar.

"What about you Sheriff? What do you care about?"

As the Sheriff went to take a bite of his omelet he paused and set his fork down on his plate.

"I care about people. People I love. People that other people love. I try to care about the people that aren't loved because they seem to need it most."

He was conflicted. "But it's subjective. I'm weighing the odds with every call I get."

"That's got to be difficult to have that kind of weight on your shoulders.

I don't know how you do it, Sheriff. I'm a nurse, but I'm not cut out for the work you do."

Fluff the ego.

"I could say the same about you. *I'm* not cut out for the work I do. But I do it. I get up and make it happen." He drank his iced tea until the ice rattled in the glass.

The Sheriff continued about the pros and cons of his life's career.

It wasn't for the faint of heart. It took guts. It also took a big chunk out of his social life and left him without much to talk about rather than rambling on about the town. That and Dorris Jean Ballard. He's a small-town Sheriff with big feelings for Dorris and every person in the community. Kat on the other hand had never been close to anyone. Except maybe the Love Doctor on late nights Friday through Sunday. Other than that Kat didn't have a social life. Just her late-night radio, and taking care of Brad.

Kat finished her second cup of coffee and the caffeine coursed through her veins and fueled her ability to focus on all the vague history of

Puckett's downfall. A hotspot for tourists and an outlet for performers and entertainers, but the town couldn't keep up with its immense growth over such a short time and suddenly Puckett went bankrupt and Jerimiah Puckett had skipped town.

"It sounds like you stay busy, Sheriff. Do you ever get a moment to yourself?" Kat quieted and hoped this would pull their conversation toward acquiring his patrol schedule type of way.

"Sometimes. Like now. The calm between storms. Thankful for slow days, but I do take time for myself. I have a deputy and he keeps an eye on things in town a night or two a week and lets me get a full night's rest."

He chuckled at something that crossed his mind.

Kat faked her intrigue as she gave the Sheriff her full undivided attention.

Two nights a week he went home to rest and his deputy took over patrol, but strictly within the town's limits. Two nights he wouldn't be snooping around the trails. She crossed her fingers in her mind.

"Only two nights? That's all?" Kat whistled.

"Hey, I appreciate the rest when I can get it. Somebody has to enforce some kind of order around these mountains or chaos would reign. Plus, we can't afford to hire anyone else and not many want to live out here. Sure, it's a pretty town and all, but it's not enough for people. No coffee shops, nail salons, dog groomers, or drive-thrus. They drive to Helen and may as well stay there." He shrugged his shoulders.

Pucket was much like a Nuclear test town, but the food was real and so were the people and the bomb itself was a black hole that sucked in your hopes and dreams.

"I hope I'm not encroaching on your downtime as valuable as it is. It's always good for your mental health to get proper rest to feel your best." She smiled sweetly as if concerned for his mental and physical well-being.

"Not at all. I'm off tonight and tomorrow and looking forward to it. I'll check in on my Aunt after we have our lunch and head home." His gaze drifted out of the big windows and down the lonesome streets toward the Bavarian home of his Aunt and Uncle.

"She will enjoy that, I'm sure." Kat smiled warmly as she mentally had begun to prepare for the picnic and pictures of the scenario unfolded in her mind as a melody hummed through the electrons firing in her brain.

If you go down in the woods today, you're sure of a big surprise.

"I try to do my best for her. She's worked hard her entire life and this is what she's earned? Don't make sense. A good woman like her." His eyes misted with the ghosts that howled wildly in his mind.

"Life in many ways is not fair. We play with the cards we are dealt and try to enjoy ourselves as we empty our pockets." Kat said as she downed the rainier of her coffee and set the erratic mug aside.

There was a null silence.

The Sheriff had gotten caught in his mournful musings and Kat didn't know where to go from there, but out the front door and to her car. Kat had what she came for and she only just needed one night.

One night with Brad.

Maryanne's senses had obviously tingled that Kat and the Sheriff's lunch session had ended as she placed the ticket for their lunches on the table, grabbed the dishes, and left.

The Sheriff reached over quickly and slid the ticket to himself, whistled sharply, and then slipped his hat back on before he stood up.

"I've got it." He winked and Kat internally rolled her eyes and smiled regardless as he joked about the heftiness of the tab that he'd picked up.

He returned as Kat stood and began bidding him adieu and thanking him for asking her to lunch. He proceeded to walk her out to her car. Her heart raced at peak rate with each step.

She stopped at the front of the candy apple red Jaguar and shined up the small silver hood ornament. The Sheriff admired her car.

"I enjoyed this. Whatever this was. It was nice talking with you, Kathy. I know you'll be heading on pretty soon after you finish your rounds, but- just be careful."

"Don't worry, Sheriff, I will be," Kat replied genuinely.

The Sheriff nodded and walked to the driver's side of the ebony Dodge Charger as Kat mirrored him going towards her Jaguar. Somehow she had refrained from dashing to the door and throwing herself behind the wheel like some mad woman.

The faster she got out of Puckett the better.

I will be careful.

Chapter Nine

Alright, get up and go, Sheriff.

Kat had driven to the motel room to wait out the Sheriff. He wasn't on her trail yet, but she knew it was best to be safe and make sure that he went home. Wherever that was because he hadn't mentioned it, at the diner he'd simply said he would be going to his Aunt's and then going *home*.

From her window of Unit 10, she could see Puckett in a wide view aside from a few buildings that blocked the site. But from her window, she could see the Pharmacy on the backside of the Ballard home. It was straight across the grass area and past the derelict teacup ride, and the west side of the community center rested to her far left. And to her far right was Floyd's diner at the corner. Far out across town from her location in Unit 10 just south of the Little Red Schoolhouse was the Judicial part of Puckett where the Sheriff's Department was located. She needed to make sure that he left Ballard's home and to take note of where he went afterward when he called home.

Kat had stood at the window for thirty minutes as she peeped out from between the gold curtains. Everything was ready to go. She'd made a few scenic stops with Brad and opened the trunk to rouse him and get some fresh air. Poor thing was tuckered out, but he held on strong. He had urinated all over brownish-yellow liquid had stained his white Lederhosen. He was dehydrated and she'd given him some water while she told him all about the picnic that she had planned for them and she had chosen the perfect spot where they wouldn't be disturbed. She really wanted to keep it a surprise, but she couldn't help herself as they had parked at an overlook.

She had gone into great detail about the sausages, honey ham, and pastries. Brad was hungry too. He hadn't eaten since he ate that bratwurst she'd smelled on his breath in the square. His eyes pleaded with her to let him have something to eat, but she chastised him and told him he needed to wait or he'd ruin his dinner and all that she had planned for him. He'd wait as long as was needed.

Brad was a champ alright.

It was almost 3:00 p.m. and the Sheriff's black patrol car left the Ballards, turned right at Floyd's, and drove along the paved road that melted into the meticulously white gravel parking lot of the Cowrock Motel. The black car rolled down the street towards the school and the red brake lights glared as it stopped and took a right.

It continued down past the park and then slowed as it pulled into a parking space in front of the Sheriff's Department.

He lives at the Sheriff's Department? Uncle Dick had mentioned he'd been previously divorced. He must have moved into the Sheriff's Department since Dorris had taken a turn for the worse and had become a human pretzel twisted in pain from the ankylosis that infested her limbs and appendages.

The Sheriff could climb up to the top of the Ferris Wheel King Kong style and shove a whole chicken up his ass and tickle his balls for all Kat cared. She'd give the Sheriff twenty more minutes and see if he left.

Quickly, she did a mental assessment of everything, the picnic basket was stocked and she had found some time to scout out to their spot and get everything just the way it needed to be. She'd disposed of the post-hole digger, gloves, and the trash she'd accumulated. She'd thrown the post-hole digger over the side of an overlook and watched it crash and splinter on its way down.

The gloves and trash were disposed of at a convenience store along the way back to Puckett. Her stomach growled as she thought about all the delicious food they'd have at their picnic because she had outdone herself this time. Usually in relationships the romance dies, but Kat wasn't going to let that happen, and was determined to stay the California Reaper she was.

Kat looked at her phone.

Almost time for the Love Doctor.

She needed to hear his silky voice tell her that everything was going to be alright. She'd attempted suicide several times in Sugardale but never succeeded. People say that if you don't succeed then you weren't doing it right, and if you weren't doing it right to begin with then you didn't want to die. But she had. She'd just wanted the torment to end. To be normal and live a normal type of lifestyle wasn't in Kat's cards. She would pull the Five of Cups every time.

The last time she'd attempted suicide was after High School had ended.

All the Seniors had graduated and moved away to go to college or to travel to Japan or Italy as a graduation gift.

Kat never got a graduation present. She'd never finished out High School and had become a pariah after she had burned down the floats that the Seniors had spent time after school hours during the semester to prepare for graduation. It was a thing that all Senior classes did in Sugardale. Some of the big wig families spent a ton of money making their spawns float the best.

Only the best for their children. Only the best clothes, and the best birthday parties for their precious babies floats that would eventually be torn apart and used for other events.

Kat had never had much money herself due to Drunk Jim, but she knew a hood ornament when she saw one. Some parents beat their children, some heavily doted on theirs, and then others showed their children off like prized cattle or a show pony. Some pedigree Schnauzer they wouldn't bother to play fetch with, but expected to perform-perform-perform. Kat knew she'd never been loved, but they weren't either and were still paraded around in public in the facade of adoration. Shiny, splendid, hood ornaments.

She'd burned those floats down, was kicked out of school, and sent to a Juvenile Prison which had been set up more like a mental institution.

The judge had tried her as an adult and sentenced her to up to two years of incarceration for Arson. Drunk Jim had refused to let her come back home that evening when she was dropped off by a deputy at the dilapidated structure.

After he slammed the door in her face she'd run to the bridge downtown and tried to hang herself, but the pants had ripped and she'd fallen down into the ravine and had to claw and climb her way back out. Then she walked disgruntled, pantless, and covered in mud back to Drunk Jim's home and had felt like more of a failure than before.

The front door had been locked of course, but she could always get in through her bedroom window and she figured Drunk Jim wouldn't have gone through the trouble of boarding up windows. Her window had opened with ease and she'd slipped inside her old bedroom that was now littered in more beer cans and bottles than ever before. She found a change of clothes in a ratty pile of some of hers that lay scattered around her room in disarray. The mattress had been dragged into the hallway and laid against the wall where Drunk Jim had abandoned the task. She had been surprised that the house was still standing. The community had come together multiple times to make sure that Drunk Jim stayed in his house and not been left to stagger around the neighborhood drunk or wind up in the Drunk Tank again. She'd found Drunk Jim passed out in his recliner in front of the TV surrounded by a sea of aluminium and glass.

The old western rerun on VHS he had been watching had ended and the old TV sets screened displayed the black and white static and race. He made quite the picture in his stained-up jogging pants and t-shirt. His dirty tube sock feet dangled from the end of the half-raised footrest of the recliner.

He had snored and scratched his belly under the glow of the television as Kat had approached. She had spied the brown bottle in his hand and like old times pried it from his sweaty palm. He began to rouse at the movement and his gaze traveled around the room in a daze until he glared up at her with such vehemence and utter loathing it had made Kat feel like the child again that had once questioned his hate for her and had yearned for a stronger paternal figure. He gritted his teeth in his polluted state of mind and had searched for something to strike her with since he had been without his favorite belt in his dingy gray sweats. His hands had lashed out at her and that's when Kat had swung the bottle at his face. He'd gasped in surprise. She'd never fought back. She'd only wanted him to love her and show her some resemblance of kindness as her figurehead.

Drunk Jim had growled and it had come out garbled as he tried to get out of the chair, but it had locked up and he had scrambled over the armrest with his arms. The apology saturated muscles in his feeble arms as he grabbed for anything he could although it had been in vain as he caught the air in front of his disowned offspring. Kat swung the bottle again and it had cracked against his cheek and left a thin red line that spread to his nostrils. His bony hands had reached to touch his face as the red line oozed down his neck. Kat reveled in the way his pupils dilated as adrenaline from fear spread across his ragged features. She'd done that.

Kat had made him feel small and afraid like he had her for so many years.

Drunk Jim had flailed in the recliner too polluted to get himself out of it as he cursed her and the day he'd ever knocked up her whore mother.

She was the lowest of the low. She was trash.

He had thrashed out and taken hold of the front of Kat's shirt and yanked her to him so close she could smell his soured sweat, the stale beer, his shit-stained underwear, and the entire unwashed length of him.

She struggled to push away from him when he had grabbed her by the throat and began to squeeze until she heard a pop. Before the pilot light in her mind fizzled out she had swung the broken bottle towards Drunk Jim and the jagged glass connected with his left jaw and he released her and fell back into the recliner with his breath coming slowly in staggered whooshes as the alcohol-soaked sponge in his skull tried to process what had happened. As she had regained her processes she had not hesitated, if she didn't end it then he would. She thought then that he'd kill her this time.

Kat had raised the bloody broken bottle over and over as it landed without rhyme or reason in the soft abdomen of Drunk Jim. With each squelch of the Drunk Jim grew less and less animated. When he could do nothing but lay and bleed in the recliner Kat went to the fridge. She'd opened the disgusting appliance and found it filled with cans and bottles amidst the forgotten takeout containers and bowls of leftovers and clabbered milk five months past Best By date. Kat had returned to Drunk Jim's side as he looked frantically around and down at his exposed guts. He'd been too preoccupied to notice her beside him, but at, her voice his head had snapped towards her.

"Are you thirsty, Jim?" He had licked his lips. He knew he was about to die and a drink would bring comfort for him until the darkness clouded his sight and he slipped into whatever Hellscape awaited him for his ways.

She had clutched four cold bottles in her left arm as she twisted the caps off and upturned the bottles over Jim's face. The amber liquid and foam had cascaded over his face and into his eyes, nose, and open wheezing gullet.

On the fourth bottle, she poured it slowly and then shoved the neck of the bottle as far down Drunk Jim's throat as she possibly could until the foam dripped from his nostrils and his flailing movements had ceased.

Kat had stepped back as the last remnants of the beer leaked down his neck and was absorbed by his dirty shirt. That was it. He'd never be able to hurt her again. But she didn't get to bask in the freedom she'd gained by closing that door without intrusive thoughts had begun to seep into and infected it with paranoia at the consequences one would pay for having done what she did to Drunk Jim. She'd just gotten out of Juvie and the next stop for her would be the Big House and big time.

So she burned that door down.

She'd taken the mattress from the hallway placed it over the stove and turned all four electric burners on high.

She'd taken one last moment to look upon Drunk Jim as he was still splayed in front of the TV ant race that illuminated the glass lodged in his mouth. One moment to rifle through his pockets for any money.

With a wad of bills and change from the TV stand in her fist, she left that house behind. The news would state later that it was diagnosed as a house fire due to negligence and that the homeowner had also tragically perished in the fire. They'd been too relieved not to have to deal with Drunk Jim's shenanigan ever again.

She'd left Sugardale and found her way around picked up a janitorial job in Atlanta at the ER and eventually saved up enough to buy herself an old car. She then lived in the car and found solace in listening to the late-night radio talks as she fell asleep in the backseat. That's when she heard his voice for the first time. The Love Doctor had been on call helping soothe all of the broken-hearted listeners out there. When she'd finally gotten a cellphone she called in and he spoke to Kat. He called her Sugar and it made her feel validated as a real person and not a burden. He was thrilled she had called in and asked what he could indulge her with, be it theraputical or musical.

The first-time caller had fallen on dead air. She'd been severely insecure all of her life and had never been asked what she wanted or what she needed by anyone and was at loss of even what song she wanted to hear played.

The Love Doctor had called out for Sugar to choose the next song that was played and she'd asked him to pick a song for her.

At that time Kat had recently discovered that Brad had died on impact in a car crash the last time she had gone to Sugardale to prowl around in her Bronco as she stalked him.

After High School and Juvie, one in the same to Kat, she kept tabs on Brad. He never got his football scholarship either. While she was away in the detention center Brad had gotten drunk and went joyriding in his car with some of his best buddies from the football team. His cronies always tagged along. He'd drunk exceedingly over the limit and had hit a lady getting into her car. His father had paid the fines and for a memorial for the lady Brad hit. But money couldn't fix a felony on his permanent record. Mr. Turner had managed to put Brad on house arrest for the entirety of his sentence, but it had cost him. The entire case had eventually cost Mr. Turner everything. Everyone was told that it was a poor stock market trade, but Brad had cost his father everything, his reputation included. The Sugardale Mall closed its doors when the bank saw red.

Months after losing not only his house, and properties, he lost his fancy car, too. Mr. Turner had enough and shot himself. Brad had continued living in the shitty trailer they'd downsized to after losing their house to the bank. After Mr. Turner turned his brain into confetti Brad lived in the trailer and lived off a small trust set up by his father until the point that he drove his car into a light pole. No seatbelt. Passersby who had witnessed the accident said he hadn't even pressed on the brakes and it hadn't taken a crime scene investigator to see it had been intentional. No tire marks leading up to the light pole.

He'd still been on house arrest and the moment he'd left his premises outside of curfew the authorities had been alerted. It had been noted as the fastest response time to any accident in Sugardale's history.

Brad was a record-setter. Brad's demise hadn't cheered her up or given her closure as she once thought it would, but his death had left a dark void inside her.

"I'm really confused about something, Love Doctor."

"Sugar, *you* can call me LD. What's got your mind in a knot? Tell *LD*." He chuckled.

"Just this guy. He's always on my mind, but he did me so wrong LD. Now he's gone and I don't know what to do." Kat had sniffled through her statement on air and the Love Doctors boys in the background *awhed* in unison.

"Look, Sugar, keep that pretty little chin up. Hard rains come before the sun shines. He did you wrong, and now you've got to *prove* him wrong. I've got just the remedy. Sugar?" He called to her over the radio waves woven with kismet cotton.

"Yes, LD?"

"Get your boots on because you are about to do some walkin'. Thank you for calling in Sugar. Stay on the line for a moment and give Maurice your information. Be aware he is a joker. Now, I've got a 105.3 *The Love Line* shirt with your name on it Sugar. It'll look sharp with them boots. Next up, *these boots are made for walkin'..*"

As the Jaguar prowled up the lane along the empty Unicoi Turnpike the night sky above was embellished with stars that seemed so close that she could reach out and pluck them out one by one and put them in her pocket.

She wound around Andrews Cove at the bend where 17 met 75.

That was their spot.

She parked on the shoulder next to a row of logs stuck vertically in the ground that dotted the side of the road around the bend of the highway. She turned the engine off and then exited the vehicle taking in a deep breath of the crisp night air.

She walked to the back of the car, pulled out a black trash bag, and then went to the trunk. She popped it open and the moonlight saturated Brad's bound hands and ankles firmly tied together so that his body curled in the form of an O in the bed of the trunk.

She saw that the chloroform in the motion sprayer was nearly exhausted of its chemicals when Brad moaned in his unconscious state. His lips were parched, cracked, and crusted with blood from near dehydration, even with what amount she'd given him during their scenic trips he'd been shut up in the trunk. Despite the cool temps outside, the inside of the vehicle retained heat, and that included the trunk and perhaps more so with Brad's combined body heat and vapors from his urine in such a confined space. Brad would get out soon enough.

"Time for our picnic. I hope you brought your appetite."

Kat rummaged through the black trash bag and removed the dirndl that she had worn in the square. She quickly got ready for Brad pulled off her sweater and slipped the leather skirt down her hips until she stood naked under the Appalachian moon. The white light bathed her naked flesh as she dressed and rebraided her hair, and then pulled the long white stockings on.

Her previous clothes were stuffed in the backseat next to the picnic basket. She'd have to come back for it. She couldn't lug it and Brad to the picnic spot. Returning to him she stood over him for a moment and noted the shallowness of his breathing. She took his ankles and pulled the rope tied around and over the side until he was hung over the lip on his stomach with his arms bent back awkwardly. His head dropped forward and his mouth had white foam caked at the corners from dehydration. She pulled on the rope that was tied around his bound wrists and ankles and his torso lurched backwards and slid down the trunk smacking his face on the bumper before he settled in the dirt facedown. Kat shook her head as she lit a cigarette and then slammed the trunk shut.

As she puffed smoke like a freight train Kat proceeded to drag Brad off of the highway and into the woods to their picnic spot. It was a chore as she hefted his deadweight through the underbrush in the dark.

In the ER and during her travel nursing escapades she would have to physically assist many of her patients. Sometimes that meant helping them from the floor after they'd fallen or even helping them to stand when their leg muscles would refuse to push them out of a chair.

Kat was stronger than she looked. She knew which way she was going now and simply buckled down and pushed through with the faint light of the moon above to guide her way.

At some point, Brad had gotten tangled in some briars around the back of his neck and with his unconscious muted state she hadn't noticed.

Right now Brad couldn't feel anything, but it would all be different once he woke up. All of the pulling and tugging on his wrists and ankles and the tension from it had popped his shoulder right out of the socket, but Kat didn't falter in her steps.

She was determined that her teddy bear had his picnic in the woods tonight.

Once she'd lugged Brad down into the woods about half a mile she let go and he seemed to congeal on the earth. His Lederhosen was covered in dirt and leaves and any exposed skin was riddled with scrapes and scratches from the underbrush and thorns. Brad remained unresponsive as she walked around the intimate clearing between a group of several large white pine trees and turned on the battery-operated LED lanterns she'd set out earlier.

Kat hummed to herself as she approached the hole in the center of the clearing around which the lanterns were encircled that cast more shadows to fill the hole that seemed to have no bottom. But it did. The hole was about five and a half feet and had taken almost five hours to dig in spans between breaks. It hadn't been easy even with the loose mountain soil.

Kat disappeared into the woods and reappeared with a twenty-five-pound bag of quick-setting concrete and then disappeared once more and came back to the hole with a second bag. She laid the top of the bag over the side and then split them wide open with a box cutter.

The pale dry mixture poured out into the hole as she retrieved a gallon of water in a clear jug and then opened and dispensed it into the hole with the concrete. She dumped the remainder of the concrete powder in and tossed the bag aside. The label bragged of mixing not being necessary. The fast-setting concrete would cure in twenty to forty minutes.

In the meantime, she walked over to Brad and loosened the knot that held Brad's bound wrists and ankles together. His feet and hands were dark blue from circulation cut off by the ropes and in such a position for nearly twenty-four hours. Even if he tried to escape now he couldn't walk properly and his hands wouldn't work. They were useless and dead now. His right shoulder was set at a weird angle beneath his Lederhosen and flopped beside his head and Kat dragged him to the hole and feet first pushed his body down into the hole and then tucked his arms snuggly at his sides. He now stood with the tops of his shoulders just reaching the mouth of the hole and his head lolled to the side.

That done, Kat hurried back to her car now able to move faster without encumbrance. She was in her car in about six minutes and took the picnic basket in hand along with her phone and cigarettes. She dashed back to the clearing in ten minutes. The concrete should be getting thicker and thicker as it congealed at the bottom of the hole and around Brad's feet and calves. She placed the basket nearby in the glow of the lanterns that cast her shadows in the trees.

The shadows danced madly as Kat unfurled the red and white checkered picnic blanket. She fluffed the checkered material over Brad's head like the giant parachute they used to flap around in P.E. at school. It caught air and glided down softly over Brad's head and the hole.

However, the picnic blanket did not conceal Brad's head as it popped through the material on the other side through a hole Kat had cut out with the box cutter. Then she set out all of the food around Brad while she hummed the jaunty tune.

If you go out in the woods today, you're sure of a big surprise.

She set the pastries to his right and the honey ham in front of him took a string of sausages and wrapped them around his neck like a scarf and his head rolled backward with his mouth agape.

She sat down on the blanket cross-legge, fanned out her dirndl's skirt provocatively, and pulled her blouse down.

She checked the time.

The Love Doctor would be on call in about thirty minutes. She slapped the sides of his face to try to rouse him. No good. His head lolled forward and he began to drool.

In situations like this one, Kat had learned to carry a *wake-up stick* otherwise known as ammonia inhalants or smelling salts. She sat up on her knees pulled a white packet from her stocking and ripped it open. She removed a white towelette. The odor of ammonia was intense as she held it over Brad's open mouth right below his nose. He sputtered as his head raised and his eyes flew loose open. Suddenly he gasped and let out a guttural yell from out of the pit as the feeling of his dislocated shoulder and dead appendages was now detected by his heavily chloroformed brain. He could feel pain. It was a most basic emotion, a feeling. He wailed, sounding like a fawn bleating for its mother, and tears and snot streamed down his face.

The smack by the bumper when she'd dumped him out of the Jaguar's trunk had knocked several of his teeth loose and some dangled by the long bloody roots. He may have bit his tongue because his words were indecipherable to a degree while speaking through globs of blood and mucus.

"Are you hungry Braddy Boo? I've got some scrumptious goodies just for you from my pic-a-nic basket."

She giggled as he struggled to move his body and whimpered in anguish at the searing pain his arm brought as the stretched skin and sinew were packed tightly inside the hole with him. The cement had begun to harden as his legs struggled in its porridge-like consistency. He opened his mouth to scream for help and Kat saw the nub of his tongue vainly waggle to make out words. He had swallowed his tongue.

"Now, stop that you've already ruined your supper. I suppose you should go without." She said this as she carved the honey ham with the box cutter. She sliced a small chunk off the ham and placed it in her mouth. She savored the salty pork. Brad had quieted his screaming and his struggle to free himself. Brad was exhausted and his limbs had failed him. His eyes studied the ham as she sliced off a second piece. If he had possessed the liquids in his body he would be salivating, but instead, his tongueless mouth quivered.

Kat berated herself for forgetting to pack any utensils in the basket so she took a stick and pierced a chunk of ham and then delivered it to Brad's trembling mouth. His head surged forward and lips enclosed around the meat. He moaned as his broken teeth began to grind the meat. He swallowed and looked for more. She did the same again and as Brad's mouth opened to invite the morsel in she saw that some of his teeth were now missing.

"Isn't this nice? Such a beautiful night. All for us."

She felt they needed some ambiance to set the mood and opened the 105.3 app on her phone. The channel opened to the end of a song as the disc jockey announced upcoming events in the area.

Kat picked up a Bavarian cream crêpe and Brad's eyes followed it as he swallowed a half-chewed chunk of ham. Brad's Adam's apple bobbed as the masticated meat slid down his dry throat. He ate like a starving dog and no longer chewed, but wolfed down everything she offered. Her phone alarm went off as it played "Mambo No. 5" which meant the Love Doctor would be on in a minute.

The music in the background continued to play and muffled the noises exuding from Brad as he dry swallowed a powdered pastry. The disc jockey on the radio signed off and introduced the Love Doctor to his audience.

His velvety voice called out to his listeners across the web of sound. He announced several sweepstakes prizes for the callers who got in line and answered a question. Kat paused the station hit the number in her contacts of the radio station and waited on a held breath as the phone line rang.

The line picked up and it was one of his boys in the background who answered each call and transferred it through to the Love Doctor.

"Hello you are Caller No. 3 tonight what's your name? Where are you from?" Kat almost squealed with excitement and trickled into a shuffling of her knees on the checkered cloth. Brad watched from his peg hole in the ground his face covered in grease, powdered sugar, cremes, and body fluids.

"Hey, LD! It's me!"

Brad started to spit out the lob of food but Kat shoved another pastry in his mouth.

"I know that voice anywhere." The Love Doctor chuckled as his boys whooped and hollered.

"Are you ready to win, Sugar?"

"You bet I am LD."

"Alright, Sugar. Which famous country singer delved into Alternative Rock as the lesser known Chris Gaines?"

Kat wasn't one to listen to country, but most people knew who Garth Brooks was, but not so much about genre-hopping days as his alter ego, Chris Gaines.

"Garth Brooks?" Kat answered the phone while Brad continued to spit bloody food out of his mouth and in her direction.

"You are correct, Sugar. Can't stump you. I'm going to pass you on to Rodrigo so I can tend to the next callers in line. Thank you for calling in. Goodnight. "

Rodrigo picked up the line and Kat hung up the phone. She hadn't gotten to speak to Love Doctor Saturday night or tonight because of the dumb sweepstakes. She called the number back and the Love Doctor crooned into the phone.

"You are Caller No.4. What's your name and where are you from?"

"It's me LD. I need to talk to you. I did-"

The Love Doctor cut her short.

"Miss Sugar tonight is the call-in sweepstakes as I stated last night. The Love Line will air next weekend on Friday night, regular hours. Now if you don't mind I need to talk to the next Caller in line. Rigo?"

The call ended as she was put back through to Rodrigo for info and shipping. Kat was infuriated and most of all deeply hurt by the brush-off from the Love Doctor. He was the only man in her life that had ever actually cared about her. She had a pile of shirts, mugs, drink koozies, glasses, keychains, and lanyards with the 105.3 logo in a storage unit in Alpharetta where she kept all of her extra belongings. Before she got the travel nurse job she had lived in the storage unit. She'd take showers at the gym down the street and she didn't need to cook anything because drive-thrus were everywhere but she kept a stocked mini fridge. It had been a decent setup until traveling and staying in nice hotels had spoiled her for finer things in life.

All of the anger she felt for LD she fed to Brad as she ripped off chunks of ham and shoved them into his mouth. He choked and vomited up all of the food she'd already fed him right in front of him and it oozed around his neck on the picnic blanket and then leaked down into the hole.

His head dropped as he caught his breath and coughed out chunks of ham. Chunky vomit covered his chin and was stuck in his mustache.

"Brad, you are a pig. Look at you. You are disgusting and wasteful. I paid for that food. Look at all I've done for you." Kat gestured to the display she had gorged him with and the empty containers scattered about the checkered blanket.

The fast-setting cement had now fully cured in the bottom of the pit and around Brad's feet. He could struggle all he wanted, but he was stuck in a position like some molded army man in green and white Lederhosen. He tried to speak, but it came out garbled, so instead he whimpered.

"Quit being such a whiny little bitch, Brad." Kat rolled her eyes as she reopened the 105.3 music app.

She'd been so infuriated about the snub by LD that she hadn't tuned back in to hear the rest of the Love Doctors session. The sweepstakes questions had been answered and the prizes had been claimed. Now, the half-hour of music without interruption ensued. The song by that one band that everyone claimed to hate, but the album sales didn't add up played in the background as Kat walked around Brad and his pit. His head seemed bodiless with the picnic blanket tucked in snug around his neck. Brad's eyes and head followed her movements and shifted left and right as she walked behind him and back around.

She stopped and then crouched down at the picnic basket. She lifted the wicker lid and removed a quart of honey from a clear mason jar with a red checkered cloth affixed to the lid. The golden liquid refracted the LED lights and sparkled like a magic elixir.

She stood and turned to face Brad. His eyes went to the jar in her hand and he shook his head and garbled "NO", but he didn't know the meaning.

Kat raised the jar over Brad's head and tipped it. The honey dribbled and oozed over his head creating a liquid bald cap and bubbled as Brad breathed through the viscous curtain. He coughed as he struggled to breathe as the stickiness invaded his nostrils and the searing sweetness coated his jagged mouth.

As the last bit dropped onto his head, Kat drug her index finger through the residue in the jar, and then brought it to her tongue.

"Mmm. Nothing like local honey to satisfy that sweet tooth."

Brad shook his head back and forth as he tried to free himself from suffocation. He blinked his honey-coated eyes and wailed loudly as he looked upwards in her direction. He couldn't see her clearly or make out anything, but a hazy figure.

LD's voice shouted out the winners for the sweepstakes again and the fury of the snub rose within Kat like a wild blaze. Brad looked up at her spitting blood and honey at her and his crude tongue tried to form the words "You bitch. Die. Bitch." That was the straw that broke the camel's back.

Kat swung the jar down on the top of Brad's skull, embedding the glass into the dome of his head. The glass cracked as Brad's head hung limp. The empty honey jar began to fill up like a phlebotomist's collection vial.

Kat took this moment to look at her work. She stood back and beheld the scene she had created.

The checkered picnic blanket was riddled with food, blood, vomit, honey, and other bodily fluids.

The LED lanterns cast a harrowing shadow over the picture she had painted and it seemed like one of those installation art pieces that depicted some foreign massacre, but oddly sweet and intimate. She hoped he had enjoyed himself with as much time as she had spent preparing this for him.

Brad never did appreciate those types of things. No meal she had ever attempted to make at Drunk Jim's had been good enough for Brad who had been born with a silver spoon in his mouth.

Kat removed her silver tin of Virginia Slims from the wicker basket, fired one up, and took a long drag.

The music app played in the basket as she set to picking up what she would dispose of and with one final glance at Brad's indulged whack-a-mole form she took the lanterns too.

"Another one bites the dust."

Chapter Ten

Monday mornings were despised by many, but this Tuesday morning felt worse than all the Mondays squashed together as Deputy Busby walked up to the red door of Unit 5 at the Cowrock.

He felt this Tuesday in particular was the lousiest for their community.

A cardboard tray balanced in his left hand Bus knocked on the door with his free one. He heard the chain rattle and the door cracked open as Fiona Peach peeped out with her blue gaze narrowed. She saw it was Bus and swung it wide open for the Deputy. The short-statured officer hurried inside the golden-fringed den of Unit 5.

He sat the tray down and quietly removed the coffees from the tray that Maryanne had fixed them and she even added whipped cream for Bus's.

Maryanne knew how to treat a man, that's for sure.

Bus had already given the others in Fiona's team their coffees at the community center. They had informed Bus of the events today.

Another body was discovered on the Unicoi Turnpike, on and scattered all around the road where 17 met 75. Wild animals had scattered pieces of a human body from a crime scene in the woods and all across the road. A car that had been driving down the road had seen the flock of vultures picking at the remnants. It had not been one for a weak stomach.

It was out of Bucky's jurisdiction, but he followed along with Fiona's team in case he could be of use until other officials could make it to the area. The call had come in around lunch time and Bucky and Fiona's team had been on the scene. The local Sheriff from Macedonia had been speaking with the witness who made the call. A middle-aged Jewish woman with two small boys in the back of her sedan. The boys watched with big eyes as the detectives, officers, and K-9 units bustled about as the scene was taped out. Fiona's team scouted the area as they flagged and bagged suspect evidence and took pictures.

Cadaver dogs from the state were requested immediately and scouted the area. The hounds had followed a trail to an open clearing of horror beneath white pines off the road.

It was dark in the undergrowth of the trees even in broad daylight, but once the crime scene had been illuminated they discovered a gore-covered hole. Bits of red and white fabric were torn to shreds like gorey confetti across the ground. This had topped Lovers Gulch whereas the moisture from the falls had washed away most of the DNA that would help to distinguish a killer. Fiona had hit a wall where evidence had been concerned.

However, off the turnpike and into the woods the air had been saturated with the stench of rotting flesh and a putrid sour odor of bile as Bucky and Fiona had engaged the scene. About five miles into the woods the forest opened where the ground was riddled with deep furrows from creature claws digging into the dirt for every morsel of carnage that was available as it had been drug through the underbrush and across the Highway like a trail of breadcrumbs.

At the center of the clearing, a dark pit gaped and siphoned the light offered by the forensic team's equipment. They discovered that the hole was about two feet in diameter and the depth was five to six feet deep, but the bottom had been filled with concrete and until it was extracted they could do no further analysis of depth.

When Bucky shined his light into the hole with Fiona close beside him the hard-nosed forensic specialist couldn't retain her revulsion at the sight below them. At the bottom of the gore-saturated hole were a pair of bloody fibula that protruded from the earth. Maggots and ants raced and wriggled across the loose ravaged flesh that hung limply from the bone. Ants crawled across the bones and chewed sinew stuck in the bottom like a burned-out candle wick. A bear or mountain lion had stuck their bodies as far into the hole as they could chew off pieces of the legs by the claw marks inside the hole. What the animals couldn't reach the ants were left and they crawled along the ground surrounding the hole and filed back and forth around Bucky and Fiona's feet.

Rats and birds had climbed into the darkness to dine on the corpse and had succumbed to the ants as well. The stench of the decomposing vermin commingled with the present odors creating a medley of derision that welled up inside the forensic detective.

As if the sight before them hadn't been gruesome enough because of the dimly lit underbrush of the forest, Fiona hadn't noticed the swarm of ants at her ankles. The insects had climbed under the hemline of her pants and attacked the soft peach flesh underneath.

Fiona was accustomed to the occasional insect bite on a scene, which was given when working in the field, but in her moment of shock the barrage of bites took her unaware and she slipped on the slick gorey mud around the hole and fell in. The fall knocked the breath from her body as she slid onto the earthy cylindrical tomb. Bucky had managed to pull her out and brushed all of the ants from her body.

She was okay now after returning and showering, but no short of shaken up.

Bus was bringing her a little happy pick me up and some cortisone ointment for the itchy ant bites. Fiona had always been like an older sister to him and he could see she was still shaken up from it. He wasn't quite sure about Fiona, but this call had been one for the books. He hadn't gone along with them, but Bus had talked to Theo, her gangly, curly-headed assistant who stayed to himself in Unit 3 and was engrossed in his computer screen as he analyzed all of the data they had gotten from the scene.

Bus had talked him into letting him in on the case details they'd pulled from the field even though Bucky had discouraged them from sharing info with his Deputy. Bucky didn't want him exposed to horrors that an officer of the law sometimes had to handle. He didn't think Bus could handle it, but Bus didn't agree. He'd bribed the computer guru with donuts and coffee from Floyd's and listened to him as he watched him scarf down all of the donuts one by one.

They'd found a mauled human skull with glass embedded in the skull the facial features chewed away and the lower mandible missing. The skull belonged to the femurs that were stuck in the concrete in the hole. The femurs belonged to the spine and rib cage that were found across the highway and the rest of the innards and organs had been strewn about by a bear or large predator. They had yet to recover the arms and might not as they considered how well the body had been picked clean.

The concrete at the bottom of the hole and femurs had yet to be recovered as they had to dig it out. The murder scene was too far out in the thick forest to send a truck so they were hiring someone to anchor the concrete with steel eye hooks and hoist it from the ground with a rope and pulley system. Manpower at its finest.

Bus wished he could be helping and pulling that block of evidence up from that pit in the ground, but he was doing his investigating.

Bucky was out on the road with the cleanup crew making sure they found anything of substance they could use to find the person who did this and why, while Fiona took a moment for herself to recuperate.

Presently, Fiona stood in front of Bus in a burgundy bathrobe with her hair wrapped in a matching terry cloth towel. Several red dots crept up her neck and more ant bites on her face, arms, and legs. She had washed all of the mud and gore from her body acquired in the hole, but the hot shower hadn't washed away the feeling she had felt inside it.

She squeezed the ointment into her palm and slathered it over her limbs and a wave of relief seemed to travel through the length of her body. Lotion returned to the table where she then sat on the end of the gold satin-draped queen with a coffee cup resting in her hands. Floyd's peach-shaped logo was embellished on the exterior of the cup. Her thumb traced the peach and over each of the letters.

"Thanks, Bus. I feel better." She smiled at the deputy who then came to sit next to her on the bed. His holster about his waist held his notepad and walkie-talkie talkie smooshed into Fiona's side and the channel opened and closed.

He readjusted and patted his friend on the back.

"Fiona, I'd do anything to see you smile. I know you might be embarrassed about falling in that hole and all, but you should see some of the situations I get myself in sometimes, and boy, I'm sure I am glad to have Bucky around."

"Yeah, I am too. I've just never experienced anything quite like that, Bus. Not falling in that hole or being embarrassed."

She sipped her coffee in thought and Bus slurped his through a straw and swirled the whipped cream throughout the cold frappe.

"I've seen homicides, murder-suicides, bodies burned beyond recognition, but I have never seen anything like this. Even Lovers Gulch had been a leap from what I've dealt with Bus. I don't know what that was in the woods, but it wasn't murder. It was evil and hateful. Who or whatever did that must have hated that person to the core. They wanted the person to be destroyed? But why?"

"Bucky's out there now getting to the bottom of it. Don't worry we will figure out who did this."

He patted his LCPD notepad and slurped his frappe.

"Well, let me get dressed. I've got to get back to the Turnpike and see what they discovered."

Bus stood up and went to the unit door stopped and looked at Fiona on the bed. She was deep in thought and not springing to get dressed.

"See you at Floyd's for dinner tonight. Take it easy, Fifi."

Chapter Eleven

Bucky ducked under the tape that blocked off the crime scenes section of the highway. He had chosen to stay on scene while the local law enforcement blocked off the highway further along.

Fiona had gone back to the motel after the catastrophe at the crime scene. He was still beating himself up for not accounting the ground could be slick with blood and guts. Her team had stayed behind and collected all the pieces they could find. The ants had ravaged what was left and had colonized the remains that were embedded in concrete. Theo and Randy took care of the ants first, but they couldn't use chemicals or it could interfere with the DNA, so instead they placed a tarp over the hole with a hose fed into the hole beneath it. Smoke was then pumped through the hose to calm the ants.

Randy wore a white hazmat suit to shield himself from the insects as he drilled eye hooks into the concrete in the hole while suspended upside down to fit into the hole. It was a tight fit. Bucky and Theo each held a leg and held Randy steady as he applied his craft. Finally, he hooked the winch straps to the eye hooks and they pulled him back out.

Once the ants had been vacuumed off the concrete and the hole sucked out and contents collected to dig through later, Bucky helped the forensic duo load up the concrete disc into the van on a wooden pallet.

The slab of concrete weighed around sixty pounds.

It hadn't been as heavy as they had thought, but the real struggle would be removing the remains from the concrete without damaging critical evidence in the process.

Whoever had committed this atrocity had thought well ahead.

Bucky slammed the van's back doors shut and slapped the side of the van. He watched Theo drive away back to Puckett's community center with the recovered evidence. There, Fiona would be prepping the lab for examination. West's Hardware in Puckett had given the team free rein of any power tools they might need to break the concrete mold. Mr. West was pretty keen on learning all the grisly details of the case as they had browsed the shelves loaded up what they needed and hauled it back to the crime lab.

The local Sheriff of Macedonia approached Bucky with a somber expression plastered to his face. He was rotund and the buttons of his uniform strained against the eye holes. His gray mustache twitched in thought as he stopped in front of Bucky. He adjusted his holster and looked around the Highway situated between the deciduous sea.

The local Sheriff was highly superstitious of the Appalachian traditions and his uneasiness was visible to Bucky.

"Bucky, I don't know what's been going on in your neck of these mountains, but it's bleeding over on my side, now. We don't have homicides like this around here. That's two in two weeks." He removed his hat and scratched his head nervously as he paced around. He shoved it back and faced Bucky.

"Look, Bob. We've got the scene all wrapped up now and Fiona's team are handling the evidence."

Sheriff Bob chuckled maniacally and the shirt buttons threatened to pop off like corn kernels.

"Yeah, I bet Floyd would be proud to see what happened today."

Bob threw a hand out towards the main crime scene where Fiona had slipped.

Anger flooded Bucky's vision and he squared up and looked the older Sheriff up and down. He could take him if it came down to it, but they had enough going to be wasting time with Bob.

"Accidents happen, Bob. I didn't see you down there helping any."

"You know what, Bucky? This whole case is way above my job description and pay grade. I get paid to pull folks over for speeding and managing traffic in the event of a wreck. I did not sign up to play scavenger hunts for jawbones and arms."

The Sheriff was at the tipping point. In the distance behind the fuming Sheriff Bucky saw a van lumber down the empty stretch of Highway. Fiona probably wanted to come check the scene out again with a collected mind.

As Bob continued on his rant the van came into focus, but it wasn't Fiona.

Great, that is exactly what this party needed.

Bob noticed Bucky wasn't paying him any mind and turned to see the news van parked beside the squad cars.

"Well, fuck me running. I knew I should have gotten my ass out of there. I can't do any more questions. I can't."

Without a word to Bucky, Bob threw his hands up in the air and made a beeline to his car, backed it up, and headed back to Macedonia.

Exasperated by the incompetence of the local police force Bucky waited for the real vultures to arrive. Lovers Gulch hadn't been enough to drag these two from their caves.

Detective Ricardo Misquera exited the driver's seat of the polished blue news van. He dusted his suit off and straightened his tie as the back doors of the van burst open and a cameraman emerged and began setting up equipment.

Misquera brushed back his lustrous ebony hair as he walked to the passenger side door and opened it.

A long-legged, blonde bombshell stepped out onto the Highway in Persian blue stilettos that matched her tightly fitted deep-necked dress. Natalie Crestburn stuck out like a sore thumb amidst the scenery.

Ricardo worked in an adjacent department with Fiona as a competitor and the powder puff Princess he tended to was the Mouth of the Mountains. They made one hell of a pair. Misquera handled the investigation details and Natalie reported the findings. They both reaped the benefits from the publicity. Natalie gained higher ratings and more viewers and it made Detective Misquera look good to the department.

Misquera seemed to nose his way into the case after everyone had done the work and took all the credit. Natalie was cut from the same cloth as she clung to the zipper of Misquera's fly and stirred as much chaos in the headlines as humanly possible. People didn't watch the news for the happy sappy stories of puppies and kittens. No, sadly, puppies and kittens didn't satisfy that psychotic nerve as the hair-raising reports that Natalie embellished upon her viewers. Her viewers didn't care if the news was factual, just that it was entertaining and removed them from their own shitty lives for a moment and that someone suffered more than them. Just for one hundred and twenty seconds of airtime

The stilettos were tattooed on the asphalt as Natalie and Misquera approached Bucky. Misquera's tailored navy blue suit and shiny black loafers stopped a few feet from Bucky. The smell of death was masked by Natalie's toilet water formula she must have drenched herself in she rolled her eyes as Bucky's own gaze looked her up and down. A life-sized blowup doll would fail in comparison.

Bucky smothered his inadvertent arousal with the derision he felt for Natalie and her counterpart, Detective Misquera.

Not much happened around here, but when it did they showed up like a nagging cough that won't go away.

"Ricky. Looks like you are late to the show this time. Where's your Mercedes? Did the ex-wife need it to drive your kids to school?"

Ricardo hissed at the nickname and the mention of his Benz and former family.

Natalie scoffed and fidgeted with her microphone and readjusted her bought and paid-for breasts in her tight blue dress.

Completely dodging the question Misquera moved closer to Bucky as he picked a fleck of dirt from under his manicured nails. His eyes moved around the scene Bucky would soon be wrapping up to allow traffic to flow back through the area.

"What happened here exactly? Another homicide like at the waterfall at the Gulch?" Ricardo straightened his cuffs. He turned to look at the caution tape trail that led into the forest. It would remain off limits for the public until further notice, but traffic could resume as usual.

"You'd think you would have done your own research before coming all the way out here."

Natalie scoffed again as she fixed her hair in the mirror of Bucky's squad car.

"We were late because that bitch had him subpoenaed for child supp-"

Misquera snapped his fingers at her and cut Natalie short. She huffed and clicked her way back to the van.

"That's none of your business. I am a part of this investigation just like Fiona is and I need details. This isn't even your jurisdiction, Sheriff."

The Colombian laughed and smoothed back his jet-black hair.

"I go where I am needed, Detective. You should probably take some notes."

Bucky said softly and Misquera watched his eyes drift over the detective's navy shoulder and towards the news van where Natalie flirted with her cameraman.

Misquera stomped off in the news van's direction to break up the tryst.

Bucky was thankful that he didn't personally have to deal with that type of relationship and went about removing the caution tape from around the scene as he heard Natalie's nasally voice. She stood perky and upbeat despite the gruesomeness of the report.

"Natalie Crestburn, here on the scene of a harrowing story that is currently unfolding along the Unicoi Turnpike. It was early this morning on Tuesday, September 12th, that a local woman was driving her two small boys to school when she discovered a grisly scene on the highway."

Her voice trailed off as he walked around rolling up the police tape on a spool and stacked the cones along the shoulder of the highway across from the crime scene trail.

The cameraman panned out to view the area and continued to film Bucky as he packed up everything into his trunk.

"Here, we have a local Sheriff wrapping up the scene to allow traffic to continue on the Unicoi Turnpike. Perhaps we can get a few words from the Sheriff."

The cameraman followed the blue bombshell as she tried to get his attention for a LIVE interview. Bucky ignored her and busily inspected the scene and relocated any forgotten equipment to his squad car to return to the forensic team.

Natalie had ceased chasing him around the highway for interrogation on air and stood for a moment smiling awkwardly into the camera lens.

"The highway will be back open soon. Good news for the community and we offer our deepest condolences to the family of the victim. Stand by for more updates, I'm Natalie Crestburn." Immediately after the cameraman angled the lens down the news reporter's smile melted.

"I don't wanna go in the woods, Ricky."

Her voice whined and Misquera winced.

He covered the distance between him and Natalie in a heartbeat placed his left hand on the small of her back and took her right hand in his as he ushered her toward the van. He tried to lower his voice but the sound carried across the highway.

"I told you not to call me that in front of officials. I'm Detective Misquera. Go sit in the van and fix your makeup. Something about your eyes they are *too*. I don' know." He waved his hands and shut the door.

He saw Bucky open his car door and hurried over expeditiously. "Wait, before you skeedaddle, Sheriff.

How far in the woods is the murder scene?"

Perspiration beaded Detective Misquera's cocoa skin above his microbladed eyebrows when he looked at the trail of death. He had probably spoken with the officers stationed at the roadblock down the highway. Misquera was charismatic where it mattered and somehow weaseled his way through life and squeezing out the juiciest details was his specialty.

He hadn't learned enough to crack this case though. Hell, Bucky wasn't sure Fiona did just yet with all of the inconclusive data rendered from the evidence.

"If you are going out there, be my guest. But there's not much in the way of evidence. I don't know what to make of it and as you said this isn't *my* jurisdiction."

That said, Bucky got in his car and cranked the engine. He tipped his hat to Detective Misquera who threw his hands up and shouted at

Natalie and the cameraman as he drove off toward Puckett.

Chapter Twelve

The community center was a beehive and Fiona was the queen bee.

Randy and Theo had knocked on the back doors and brought in all of the evidence collected on the scene.

Bus had set up a sturdy metal table for the concrete block and once Randy rolled the palette in through the doors they went to work to remove the feet without damaging them any more if possible.

A circular saw with a diamond abrasive blade did the job as Randy chipped away pieces of concrete and they fell to the floor where Bus with a white Uline dust mask and a broom and dustpan diligently swept the dust and rock into the pan and dumped it in a trash bag.

Fiona stood close by Randy with safety glasses and a digital voice recorder as she declared post-mortem discovery.

"Object in discovery is a fifty-pound block of cement removed from a six-foot hole in mountain terrain. Buried in the concrete are two human feet with a partial fibula still attached and covered in a mesh fabric or hosiery."

Fiona paced around the table as Bus danced around sweeping up debris. Theo took pictures as Fiona directed for the report. She studied the matter at hand as Randy freed the remains. A pair of dismembered feet in what had once been white socks. Fiona snipped away the fabric and they then laid before her like ripened monstera. The toenails had been peeled back from the beds and had been stuck in the chipped pieces of concrete through the fabric.

"Where the concrete that had encased the dismembered appendages the drying agent in the concrete mixture has absorbed all of the fluids. Skin is blistered from heat of drying agents and underneath the material, the flesh is gray, dry, and flaking off."

Fiona picked up a pair of long tweezers in her purple latex-gloved hands. She plucked a piece of the tissue from the ankle and held it beneath a light. She then dropped it in a clear sample baggie that she handed off to Randy. He was finished with the circular saw and now printed the evidence information in the report as Fiona handed it off to him. Fiona was in her Flow State. She was primed, focused, and confident in her process.

"Feet are determined to be male. Both the fibula and tibia in each foot have been disjointed by great force."

Theo snapped several pictures and then moved out of the way.

"Intact fibula and tibia measure seven and a quarter inches. The victim is estimated to be around five foot five to six feet tall. Probable weight is around one hundred fifty pounds to one seventy-five."

Fiona slipped on a headlamp with a magnifying lens attached and moved closer to the examination table. She cut a striking picture in with her headlamp, white mask, and full apron.

"Protruding fibula and tibia shows signs of post-mortem trauma sustained from large animal bites. Rodents have gnawed at the remainder of the bone. Ants colonized inside the bone mass."

Fiona worried at her ant bites. She then took a scalpel, dug out a sample of congealed bone marrow, and then scraped it into a glass container. Randy took it, recorded the info on the label sticker, and then set it with the other samples.

Bus stood back and watched Fiona complete her discovery.

"There appears to be a fiber embedded in the bone." Randy retrieved the sample baggie that contained the small red thread.

"Joints had sustained injury antemortem as if restrained before death." Fiona quieted and stood before the table.

Bus watched enamored as she gestured to Randy who rushed over and began to cut a thin sample of the remains off for examination under a microscope.

As the circular saw whirred on and its metal teeth began to bite into the bone, Bucky walked through the front doors and Fiona's face lit up when she saw him, but he noted her stern expression surface in the shadow of the case.

"Hey, Buck." Bus waved from Fiona's office chair where he had taken up station to watch the Forensic team in their fluid second nature movements. They worked like a finely tuned machine together and had the evidence bagged and labeled and would be soon onto the next step of the forensic analysis.

At his computer, Theo put everything together in the program he had created for the team's case file. It was quite impressive for a college dropout she met in a True Crime podcast feed online.

Once Theo uploaded all of the pictures and data entries and once each piece of flesh, bone, and fabric was challenged beneath her microscope's lens then the program's algorithm went to work. It would compile all of the evidence for them into a pristine presentation and would also red-flag corresponding anomalies. His program took all of the hours spent shuffling case files to compare notes and sifting through the crime scene photos and ultimately sped the process up a hundredfold.

Fiona removed her gloves, headlamp, and apron as she talked to Theo and Randy.

"Guys, I'm going to go get us some lunch at Floyd's and talk to Bucky.

Any special requests? Speak now or forever hold your peace." Fiona slipped on her jacket over her long-sleeved black shirt and jeans and quickly grabbed her tablet.

"Maryanne will know exactly what I want. Just watch." Bus said smugly.

"I'll take a plain burger, meat and cheese only, fries, and a sweet tea," Randy said as he bagged up the feet to place in the van's built-in freezer, or as he called it a mobile mini morgue.

Theo was too wrapped up in his laptop's screen to answer as his fingers typed at lightning speed, but Fiona knew his shtick, chicken fingers, fries, and a milkshake. Nothing extraordinary, but he could eat it easily as he worked.

Outside they talked as they walked to Floyd's. Fiona opened Theo's program and she could see all of the info that they had already collected and had been uploaded. It was updated in real time as Theo uploaded photos and files. Randy would start analyzing each piece of evidence that they had bagged at the crime scene and Theo would upload it. In the program, all of the crime scene photos were there and Fiona swiped through them one by one. Bucky walked beside her and looked at the screen as she enlarged an image of the feet stuck in concrete after being hoisted from the pit.

"You should take a break, Peach." She shushed him and he grinned as he knew before saying it that she wouldn't agree. Fiona had a one-track mind and it was hauling justice.

"Bucky, I've told you before, I'll sleep when I'm dead. It doesn't look like anyone else sleeps." Fiona chided as she opened a file on the details of the case.

Theos program had computed her voice recording of her discovery into text and applied the program to it. Once everything was uploaded the algorithm would allocate pictures and information into a smooth report with history gathered from DNA, and businesses associated with the victim, complete with contact details and addresses. It hadn't failed the team yet since Theo put the program to use. They'd nailed every perpetrator that crossed them and in less time. Eventually, after Theo got everything the way he wanted it he hoped to share it and help solve cases around the world.

They passed by the motel where Siley's car sat alone in front of the establishment and Fiona's suburban still was parked in front of Unit 5.

"It's going to take a few weeks before we get back anything once we send it in. I don't have much to work with here. The wildlife did a number on the guy. All I have is feet and bits and pieces."

Fiona closed the screen out as they were yards away from the diner.

She sighed and looked over at Bucky. He was in deep thought, a stern expression twisted his features.

"There's got to be something there. We bagged up everything we found."

"I know Buck, but sometimes it's not enough like with Aaron Michaels. We had dental records, medical, work history, and everything in between. Hell, we even found child pornography on his laptop and it was hidden well.

Still nothing." She looked disgusted and threw her hands up in the air.

Bucky stopped short of the diner's front doors. He looked over at Fiona and shook his head.

"You need a break." He said as he opened the door for her.

"No, I don't." She narrowed her blue eyes at him and then stomped through over the threshold.

They were right on time in the peak hours of the lunch rush as they took a seat to give Mrs. Flora and Maryanne a chance to get the others' orders out. Bucky tipped his hat in Maryanne's direction as she rushed past with hands full of empty dishes.

"I'll be right there, Bucky. Hey, Fifi!" The redhead called to them as she disappeared into the kitchen. Other patrons looked their way, some waved, some nodded their way, and others whispered to each other.

No matter Fiona's history in Puckett and how well she was liked by everyone, they still felt uneasy around her as someone who frequently spent time with the dead, or pieces of the dead. and by choice of reason.

As superstitious as the mountain folk were in Puckett, anything more would tip them over the edge. It was something Fiona had grown used to and accustomed to over the years. She enjoyed the seclusion of her work and contrary to belief felt comforted by the dead. Maybe not the horrendous odors or the sight of a body in active decay, but the affirmation of her life. She was alive and that was more than she could say for her clients.

Fiona yawned and Bucky noticed.

"I'm not saying take the whole year off, Fiona. Take tonight off. Randy and Theo have it under control and you can get right back to it in the morning. Get some sleep tonight, Peaches, or you are going to run yourself into the ground."

Fiona huffed at Bucky for suggesting such a thing.

Maryanne came around and took their orders and while they waited Fiona checked the program again. Theo was still entering data. She closed the tablet and looked at her reflection on the black mirror's screen.

As much as she hated to admit it, Bucky was right. She needed a break. Fiona wasn't one for dolling herself up with layers of foundation and lacquering her lips with petroleum gloss. She chose a casual presentation to her appearance that was professional, but she didn't have the time nor the patience for a cosmetic routine.

"Okay. Maybe one night." Bucky grinned with satisfaction.

"But I'll be back at it tomorrow. First thing." She looked away from his mirthful gaze and outside the diner. The parking lot was emptying as Maryanne showed up with their orders in plastic bags and then left to return with their drink orders in cardboard cup holders.

"I put everything in the bags. There are extra napkins, straws, ketchup, mustard, and some other sauces. I fixed Bus five grilled cheese sandwiches and those little gherkin dill pickles that he loves, and a milkshake with extra whipped cream." She giggled and then left to clear a table.

As Fiona peeped into the bags Bucky leaned forward across the table and said in a low husky voice. "How about we take this back to the boys and then we can finish discussing this at the Rock?"

Fiona paused and stared up at Bucky with her own devilish grin.

After they delivered lunch and informed the team that she would be retiring early to get some much-needed rest, Fiona and Bucky took their lunch and headed to the Cowrock. Randy and Theo had agreed and assured Fiona that she need not worry and that they would get all of the evidence processed. She would be ready tomorrow and with a fresh set of eyes after such a gruesome morning.

As Fiona took a moment in the Unit's bathroom, Bucky bolted the door, closed the curtains tightly, and fluffed up the pillows on the queen-sized bed that resembled a golden bullion. He turned the TV on for background noise as he heard Fiona open the bathroom door. He turned and his pants suddenly got tighter below his gun holster as Fiona stood in nothing, but a black lace bra and panties. She nervously moved under his gaze and looked down at her bare feet.

Bucky crossed the room in a few strides, picked her up, and carried her to the bed. He laid her down like a fragile doll that had been broken too many times before.

She lay vulnerable and under the iridescent lighting, Bucky saw the thin white scars along her wrists that she kept covered with long sleeves or coats. Other scars across her body for other reasons and each had a story. They told the story of Fiona's life. All the cigarette burns from her mother when she would speak out or say something rude to one of her male friends, especially to the touchy grabby ones.

Bucky bent down at her ankles as she lay back against the gold satin pillows, and Fiona moaned as he kissed every scar with such tenderness it made her eyes well with emotion. He kissed her knees and trailed up along her inner thighs until his warm breath heated the fabric of her lace panties. His eyes searched hers as his index finger slid under the lace hemline and delved into Fiona's velvet underground. Her back arched and Bucky pulled the fabric down over her thighs revealing a manicured lawn guarding the gates of paradise. He kissed the tops of her thighs as he slid the fabric down to her knees and then nibbled along her pelvis and soft abdomen.

When his tongue slid between the lips and tickled her nerve endings Fiona's hands grabbed Bucky's head and shoved his face into her most vulnerable bits. Her thighs squeezed his ears as he dined on the Georgia peach wrapped around his face in a vice grip.

She writhed against the gold bedspread as Bucky's mouth drove her over the cliffs of insanity into that moment of ecstasy where all the thoughts that constantly raced through her mind stopped and faded away in a vibrational haze.

When Fiona's thigh grip loosened Bucky raised on his knees and removed his uniform shirt and then his hands went for his holster, but Fiona's hands were already there as she unbuckled the leather belt and freed the throbbing prisoner from its cell.

Before Bucky could remove his pants Fiona grabbed it firmly at the base and slid the tip into her mouth tasting the salt, sweat, and masculine energy that exuded from the veined flesh. She caressed and cradled his balls as she took more of Bucky into her mouth. She felt him alive in her mouth and as she looked up at him he placed his hand on her shoulder and pushed her back against the bed and his body followed hers in perfect harmony.

Fiona unhooked her bra, and as the black lace fell, her milky white breasts contrasted against the tan lines from working out in the field. His hands explored her body as if he'd never seen it before. He caressed her breasts and pinched the pink erect nipples gently. He received small breathless moans from Fiona. When his hard shaft entered her she gasped and arched to meet each of his thrusts. He flipped her over on her stomach and grabbed her firmly by the hips as he pulled her to him over and over.

Her black hair was tossed back as she took in every inch of Bucky. He pressed her face further into the mattress with each thrust. He flipped her back around, threw her left leg over his shoulder, and continued the timeless rhythm of carnal pleasure.

Fiona braced herself on her elbows as Bucky lowered his head and took an engorged nipple into his mouth. His strokes slowed and Fiona felt him stiffen more as the girth pressed inside of her. Their eyes locked as Bucky pulled himself from Fiona and moved over her until his balls drug between her breasts and he released his load into Fiona's awaiting mouth. She was eager to receive every last pearly bead and when one settled on her chin, she scooped it off with her finger and then stuck it in her mouth. Bucky laid down beside her, pulled her naked body to his, and covered them both with the gold satin flat sheet.

They lay close together with arms and legs entangled. Bucky brushed back the hair from Fiona's face as she nestled into his chest and drifted off but sleep did come so easily for Bucky.

After Fiona fell asleep Bucky got dressed and stepped outside of the motel room and into the brisk night air. He wasn't one to smoke, but in a session like that, he felt the craving for nicotine heavy on his tongue. He could still taste Fiona and it immediately brought back the feeling of her thighs wrapped around his head and his flesh sliding into her tight, wet embrace.

He stood outside the Unit wishing Quickies was open at this hour he heard the door to Unit 10 shut and the nurse stood admiring the quiet scenery and graveyard of fair equipment that surrounded them. The giant Ferris wheel loomed in the distance and sat like a forgotten rusted giant. The nurse saw Bucky and then walked over towards him as she bundled up in her sweater against the chill night.

"Good evening, Sheriff," she said as she pulled a metal tin from her pocket, flipped it open, and freed a cigarette from the case. She placed the white butt in her lips, flicked the flint, and a flame emerged and licked the tip of the cigarette hungrily. The aroma of tobacco invaded Bucky's nostrils.

"Do you mind? I don't usually smoke, but Quickies is closed."

She smirked with the cigarette between her lips as she fingered another cigarette from the tin. She then stuck it in Bucky's mouth and lit it.

He pulled the smoke into his lungs and exhaled a cloud when the nicotine hit his bloodstream. The wind carried the cloud away across the white gravel and dissipated.

"Menthol." He said but settled for another drag.

"Long day at the office, Sheriff?" She puffed her cigarette and hugged the sweater tight to her body. She looked sideways at Bucky and he sighed.

"Something like that." Bucky laughed to himself. A long day? Only a day? If only she knew what horrors they had witnessed in the past week. However, Kathy Walters was a seasoned nurse and had probably seen her fill of death.

"Well, it all starts over again, tomorrow. It never ends." She brushed away blond wisps the breeze had pushed across her face from the gusts that rushed up the mountainside and across Puckett. The view over the cliffs was mesmerizing. The lights of the cities that stretched out for miles before them looked like lightning bugs blinking in the distance.

"Yeah, I know. I am hoping tomorrow that it ends."

Kathy stiffened and then looked at him from her peripheral. He took the last drag from his cigarette and knocked the cherry out and stuffed the dead butt into his pocket to throw away. Siley would appreciate it and not have to collect all of the butts by hand from the stones.

He rested against the wall while he viewed the town he had sworn to protect. Seemed like he never had time to work on the things in town that needed to be done especially now with the bodies they had recovered. Or parts they had scavenged.

"Don't beat yourself up, Sheriff. You are probably closer to cracking this egg than you think. I've seen the new reports on TV and online. Looks like I picked a terrible time to come stay."

"It's part of the job description. Too many factors play into it and it's difficult not to blame myself. As for your stay here, it may be badly timed, but I appreciate the work you do and have done for my Aunt. I figure I can't begin to comprehend the things you've seen in your career."

"It's part of the job description, Sheriff. I take each client as they come and try to relax in my downtime. Life is short and sometimes unfair.

Better to enjoy the time you have left while you got it."

"Yeah." Bucky smoothed out the gravel with his shoe.

"Well, I had better get to bed, conference call early in the morning for me. Goodnight, Sheriff." She nodded and walked back to her Unit and left Bucky to his musings.

Chapter Thirteen

Bucky was with Fiona and that left Bus on patrol. In his squadcart, he cruised around the park and past the Little Red Schoolhouse as he checked for any hooligans out and about after business hours, but the streets were calm and desolate of people. Fall was in the air as leaves stirred across the ground picked up by the swift mountain breeze and his radio spilled out music from 105.3's station when he turned down Main Street. He kept the volume down enough that he wouldn't disturb anyone, but the music helped pass the time at night. It felt spooky tonight as he patrolled under the waning moonlight. Perhaps he was on edge after witnessing the crime scenes firsthand. But he had to push that all out of his mind. He had to prove to Bucky that he could handle the job details of an officer of the law. He could take care of himself.

Bus drove the squadcart around the corner by Floyd's and then up the street by the Cowrock. Nothing to see there. Everything was quiet.

The Forensic team had finished up at the community center and retired to their units. He drove by the rusty fair equipment and shined a light around to make sure someone hadn't taken up residence in one of the rides or vendor stalls. Everything looked good to go.

He drove around the backside of the community center to secure that area and hopped out of his cart to check that the doors were locked. They were nice and secure. That eased Bus's mind and he strolled back to the East side of the building where he stalled the cart.

Across the way, he saw a shadowy figure emerge from the shadows at the back of his parent's home. He stayed back and waited for the figure to come into view.

Under the streetlights, Bus made out the figure to be a woman and blonde. She walked from Ballard's home. He kept his eyes on her as she continued towards the motel and then into the last Unit. That had to be the nurse that was caring for his mother. Bus had been relieved to see her of all people. He hadn't gotten to introduce himself, but his father had spoken very highly of her.

Nothing to see here.

The next morning, Bus was ready to go. He'd already swung by Floyd's to see Maryanne and fill his belly with some of Mrs. Flora's pancakes. His mother didn't cook breakfast anymore since she became so sick. His father usually took up the duty of cooking breakfast, but last night his mother hadn't slept all night because of the pain and torment her prison of a body had become. That would explain why he had seen the nurse leaving his parent's home. It upset Bus a great deal even while his father and Bucky tried to shield him from seeing her in that state. That's why he and Bucky had moved into the station.

Bucky made it work. They had empty cells that they had claimed as their rooms since they had never seen many criminals held before but were usually transferred to Macedonia. Bucky said they were testing out the cells for official purposes and Bus was too eager to assume responsibility for such a grand project. He missed his mother's cooking dearly, but Mrs. Flora's was the next best thing and the two officers ate there at breakfast, lunch, and dinner.

Now, Bus was back on duty and passing out citations for those parking incorrectly. So far there weren't any violators and that wasn't a bad thing.

That just meant that Bus was doing his job. He was proud to see his perfectly drawn parking parameters were being utilized effectively.

Bucky would be patrolling tonight around the highways and Bus would stick around to secure the town limits. Bus drove around the town's streets a few times and waved at all the familiar faces he saw as they went about their daily routines. After he was satisfied that the streets were safe he rolled over to the community center to see how the team was performing today. As soon as he opened the doors he saw Fiona staring into the screen of her high-powered comparison microscope. On the screen were tiny lines. Bus wasn't sure what she was looking at, but it sure looked interesting to him. He moved in closer for a look and pulled a candy bar from his lapel pocket.

"Hey, Bus," Fiona said as the Deputy stood off to the side to watch her while he snacked on his candy bar. Randy and Theo greeted Bus from Theo's station in front of his computer where they were putting in new data from Fiona's analysis. The crate next to Fiona held the remaining evidence baggies from the crime scene that she had yet to analyze under her magnifying lens.

"What are you doing now, Fiona?" He bit a piece from his candy bar as he leaned in closer to look at the thin lines on the screen.

Fiona sat back and stretched his arms over her head and looked over at the deputy.

"Where's mine?" Her eyes landed on the candy bar and Bus's face went pale for a moment.

"I'm just picking with you. I don't even have an appetite at the moment." She sighed and looked back at the screen. Bus was relieved. He'd always been taught that if you didn't have enough to share with the class then you needn't bring anything at all. He was learning here so it may as well be class.

"I'm currently analyzing a fiber that was found embedded in the white stocking on the feet during the discovery. I compared it to hairs that were still attached to the ankles and it's not a hair from the victim, an animal, or clothing."

"It's not from the crime scene either," Randy said from beside Theo.

"No, it's not. It could be from the assailant. But I still am not sure what it is. I found other pieces of cloth from what appeared to be a red and white checkered cloth. It was chewed up."

"A picnic blanket," Bus said as he chomped on the last bite of his bar.

Fiona's eyes lit up. She picked up her tablet, swiped through all of the uploaded evidence, and pulled up the image of the cloth.

"Bus, you are a genius. Why didn't I think of that?" She computed all the info into her notes.

Bus grinned and puffed out his chest with pride.

See, Bucky didn't have anything to worry about and he could be an asset to the team if they'd give him a chance.

"That makes sense since we found pieces of food that the animals and bugs didn't carry off and a hambone. A picnic that went wrong?"

They all quieted as they considered the notion.

"Ain't no picnic without the food," Bus said as he walked to the fridge and pulled out a bottle of water. He twisted the top and took a long swig.

"I think you're right, Bus. Polyester fibers. But what happened? The victim was planted in the hole with concrete. I looked at that too and it contained calcium chloride, an accelerator in fast-setting concrete."

Fiona swiped through the images on her tablet and then to the abrasions on the chewed fibula.

"Which means it took around forty-five minutes to cure and harden. Meaning it took twenty minutes for the victim to be dragged through the woods and put into the hole. The cement hardened skin tight to the victim's lower appendages and with no wiggle room which leads me to believe that the victim was unconscious prior to being placed in that hole."

Theo said from his desk as he typed in data. He may not appear to be involved in their discussion, but Theo was very aware of what was being said even though his attention seemed focused on the task at hand.

At a young age, Theo had been diagnosed with Asperger's syndrome and struggled with socializing in school where his parents had paid for private tutoring at home and he had become hyper-fixated on the then-new high-end active matrix LCD PowerBook 500.

The Powerbook 500 became Theo's gateway into the digital realm and later would be the cause of his expulsion from the University after leaking all of the files of the students who harassed him every day between classes and how he met Fiona through an online True Crime group.

"And can we talk about the hole itself? Five and a half feet to be exact and two feet in diameter." Randy said as he walked to stand by Theo who had instantly retrieved the image from its file folder and displayed it on screen.

Theo grunted in agreement as all four of them fanned out behind his chair. The image shown was of the concrete prior to it being destroyed to free the feet.

The concrete disc's bottom was shown as Randy and Bus held it steady for Theo to snap a picture. The concrete had created a plaster mold to the shape of the jagged furrows in the ground beneath it.

"Shovel?" Randy said as he leaned in closer."

"Wouldn't the furrows go in one direction if it were a shovel? These marks are nearly uniform." Fiona questioned.

"Yeah, unless the killer walked around the hole digging in different directions. It looks like it was dug with a set of post-hole diggers." Randy said quietly as he shook his head and Bus whistled.

"What?" Fiona asked, looking at Bus and Randy.

"That took some dedication there."

Randy chuckled at his dark humor.

"I dug a hole with some post-hole diggers once to plant a tree beside the house when I was little and it took me forever. Mom was proud of me. Only took me two days after school." Bus said proudly and adjusted his belt and holster.

"Suppose the killer had been prepping this for a while and dug the hole over a period of days," Theo added.

"That seems possible. People go to Andrew's Cove all the time to hike and camp. Any number of people could have gone through there and stayed for a week or so."

Fiona rubbed her eyes and looked away from the screen. Her eyes were strained from the endless analysis. Too much evidence had never been an issue, but her eyes and brain pleaded with her.

She'd power through like always.

"We can check into the registry and see if anything sticks out. I also noticed these abrasions on the posterior of both fibula and it appears the victim had been bound before being put in the hole. By a rope that dug into his soleus so hard that hair follicles and tissues were lodged into the bone."

The image showed bone riddled with teeth marks and where Fiona's finger pointed beneath the layer of scrapes and bite marks.

There was a rough circular abrasion on both fibula.

"However, the abrasions were deeper on the anterior ankle."

"As if the rope were pulled intensely and with some force." Randy expanded on the idea. "It couldn't have been attached to something outside the hole. There aren't any drag marks resembling a rope."

"Well, if there was a rope, and once the victim's legs were eaten, then the rope would have slipped off."

Randy nodded his head pleased with the conclusion they had reached together.

"I'll tell Bucky to be on the lookout for the missing rope. We could have missed anything out there with the way the wildlife crashed the scene.

Bus squinted at the screen over Theo's shoulder as he blew up an image of the skull that was recovered.

"Good Lord Almighty!" Bus's eyes widened at the gruesome display. Some things weren't meant to be seen, but he had a job to do and it was better for him to see it than someone else. He had to be one of the few to have witnessed this atrocity.

The skull was fragmented and covered in bite marks. All of the connecting flesh and skin has been generously picked over by animals and bugs.

"There is a hole at the top of the calvaria in a circular shape. Seems like the killer might have had an obsession with circles. Shards of glass were found in the wound and remnants of glucose and fructose stuck to them. We have determined the glass is from a jar of honey. A Ball mason jar."

"There are over one hundred bee farms and honey distributors in the state of Georgia alone. It would be near impossible to narrow it down unless we find a jar and possibly a label of some kind." Said Theo matter-of-factly.

"We didn't recover a jar. An animal probably carried it off too. We didn't even find the dirt that came out of that hole. There should have been a pile of it around somewhere."

Fiona exclaimed as she sat down in her chair and rubbed her temples. Her brain was turning to soup. What was so different about this crime from all of the others? She felt thrown off her game and left in the open. The scene at Lover's Gulch was pretty gnarly too, but perhaps it was because she fell in that pit and it made her feel helpless. The ant bites had stopped itching, but the embarrassment had not subsided.

It wasn't as if Fiona fell thrown off because the case had frightened her or was it too much for her to handle. At this point, Fiona could eat a ham sandwich and perform an autopsy at the same time, and use the body's chest as a dinner plate. No, the blood and guts didn't phase her, but it was the preparation that made her hair rise on end.

Chapter Fourteen

Bucky was on his way to a call to where a ranger was waiting eight miles South of the Unicoi Turnpike's crime scene. He parked behind the Ranger's SUV and got out to meet Todd Colhon and find out what was going on. The ranger hadn't been clear on the reason but said it was urgent and figured Forensics should probably take a look too. He'd quickly added that he had tried to contact Fiona first, but his call wouldn't go through.

"Evening, Sheriff. Thanks for getting here so fast." He shook Bucky's hand, hurried to the back of the SUV, and opened the hatch.

"I apologize for not explaining the urgency, but I just tranquilized an eight-hundred-pound bear to remove a rope it had gotten tangled in. Suppose that didn't have my heart pounding enough. I didn't expect this." Colhon opened up a plastic bag and then sidestepped for Bucky.

Bucky stepped into view of the opened hatch of the vehicle. He saw the tangle of rope and bone in the plastic bag as the stench stung his olfactory senses. The sickly sweet odor of death hung in the air as he backed up without a word and took his walkie from his belt.

"Bus, pick up. Over."

The Ranger watched him and stepped back leaving the hatch open to air out from the stench.

"Hey, Bucky! Over!" Bus exclaimed excitedly over the walkie-talkie's staticky channel.

"Where are you now?" Said Bucky.

"I'm over here at the community center. I mean crime lab. Over!"

"Bus, now you know I told you not to get involved in these cases. That's beside the point. Bus, I need you to tell Fiona-"

"She can hear you, Bucky."

"Okay, Fiona, you need to get down here to the Turnpike ASAP, but call me when you get reception and I'll explain more over the phone. Something turned up."

"Okay, we are on our way. Talk to you soon." Fiona confirmed over the walkie-talkie."

"Over! She forgot to say Over. Over!"

Bucky returned his attention to Ranger Colhon who looked green around the gills.

"So what happened here? You found it?"

"I received a report that a black bear had been sighted in the area.

We recently had an influx of campers at the Cove with Oktoberfest just beginning in Helen. They are told to leave the campsite better than they found it, but do they listen? The bear went on a spree over the past few days knocking over trash cans and terrorizing the campers. But the report said the bear had something wrapped around its neck.

I finally saw him today and it took five tranqs to get him down."

The Ranger sighed heavily, took out his phone, and waved Bucky over.

"I don't know if it helps, but I managed to get a picture while he was down. My hands were shaky. That was the biggest black bear I have ever seen around here. They don't usually get over five hundred pounds." His face went pale at the recollection.

"Send those pictures you took to my cell and I'll make sure that Fiona gets them. She should be here soon."

Fiona, Randy, and Theo arrived on the scene ten minutes later and were ready to break down another crime scene.

Fiona approached and Bucky discreetly winked at her as she walked by to view the discovery, but Fiona was zoned in and in motion as she began a quick analysis of what was recovered. All work and no play.

"Randy, can you get that in the van while I talk to Ranger Colhon."

Randy quickly went to work removing the burden from the Ranger vehicle as Fiona pressed for any more details that she thought Bucky hadn't thought to ask.

"Where is the bear now? You captured it?"

"I released the bear. I tranqed it to untangle it from the rope. Wildlife is always released back into the wild. Capture and release. Is there a problem?" The Ranger said with a tremble in his voice as he felt he may have handled the situation wrong in Forensic terms. He was young and probably helped maintain Andrews Cove and didn't spend his time untangling bones from historic-sized black bears.

Fiona studied the contents of the plastic bag.

"Yes. But, no. I'd pay good money to see the contents of that bear's stomach."

The Ranger swallowed a lump that had caught under his Adam's Apple as he straightened his hat.

"It's stomach?"

"You do know that there was a murder nearby here don't you Ranger Colhon," Fiona said in a somber tone while she removed her purple latex gloves and stashed them in her pocket.

The young Ranger nodded and shifted uneasily under the Forensic investigator's unyielding gaze.

"Yes. Well. I heard about it on the radio. 105.3 didn't have much information."

"There was a murder and this bear that you found is a suspect. Bear or not."

Fiona said as she looked off behind the Ranger and into the woods.

"You want me to arrest the bear, ma'am? I don't think I can do that."

The Ranger looked at Bucky for help with such a request.

"No, do not arrest the bear. But it should have its stomach pumped. It's been eating trash so you may as well. There was a bear in Colorado that almost starved to death from trash blocking its intestines. The black bear you released could still have crime scene evidence in its stomach."

The Ranger looked nauseated at the notion.

Randy returned from the van and heard the conversation details as he walked up.

"I don't think that will do any good. The contents of the bear's stomach would have probably metabolized by now and with everything it's eaten since the murder. Does a bear shit in the woods?"

"Frequently." Ranger Colhon stated with disgust at the nature of the discussion. He looked at Fiona and her team, Theo included, as he remained in the van bent over his laptop in deep focus. They were a strange crowd for conversation.

"You're probably right, Randy. It just seems like the closer I get the farther the truth runs." She turned to the Ranger.

"Nix the stomach pumping. Thanks for your service today, Ranger Colhon."

She shook his hand and turned her attention to Bucky.

"Will you be heading back to Puckett after this? We are going back to see what he found and what to make of it."

"I'll head back that way soon."

Bucky assured Fiona. She nodded and got in the van's passenger as Randy took the cockpit. They then headed back down the Unicoi Turnpike with Bucky soon to follow.

Back in Puckett the team had quickly gone to work on the new evidence and were thirsty to find the source of the crime. Bucky showed up to see Randy, Fiona, and Bus standing around the makeshift examination table.

Displayed on the table were the rope, three long bones, and a large evidence baggie.

Bucky approached the table.

"What do we have here?" He said as he edged around the table near Fiona with her headlamp and retractable magnifying monocle.

"What we have here are two sets of radius and one ulna. One end of the bones have been chewed off from the point of reach the bear had as they hung from its neck."

Fiona picked up the mauled radius that once comprised the victim's forearm.

"So the victim was bound."

"Yes, the victim was bound. These bones have the same abrasions that the feet had and it's the same type of rope that was found on the deceased Aaron Michaels at Lover's Gulch."

They had already been discussing the similarities between both murder cases when Bucky arrived.

"You're saying it's the same killer at both sites?" Bucky said to confirm his thoughts.

"Yes. The same rope material as the other crime scene."

Fiona nodded to Randy who held up a plastic baggie with the rope from Aaron Michaels's murder.

"We have a serial killer on our hands for sure. The abrasions on Aaron Michaels's bones match the ones on our John Doe's feet."

"Don't forget the homemade chloroform in the bone marrow. The guy must have been swimming in it." Randy added from the corner of the examination table.

"The residual levels that remained were substantial since normally chloroform doesn't stay in the bloodstream long. As Randy said, the victim must have been drowning in it."

"What does that mean now?"

Bus asked and Bucky looked at his cousin with worry. Bus was stubborn, but that was to be admired. As much as Bucky put walls up around Bus to protect him, the quicker he scaled those walls to prove himself.

"That means that we have found the killer's signature, rope, and homemade chloroform."

"But we still don't have a motive. The killer hogties the victims, tortures them, and then kills them in brutal ways. First by drowning in the Gulch and then mauled by a bear in a hole."

"Technically, John Doe could have died prior to the bear by the honey jar," Theo added from his desk as he uploaded new evidence data into his program.

"True." Fiona agreed.

"Can't you find out where the honey came from? Who manufactured it?"

"No, not without the jar. There are over a hundred beekeepers and honey vendors in the state of Georgia not factoring in honey from out of state. Dead end there."

"Where do we go from here?" Bucky asked the pensieve investigator.

"We finally got a call back from Jerry Jenerals Regional Supervisor who worked with Aaron Michaels. She claimed that Aaron had filed complaints about harassment from a customer. Multiple times. She said she would email over the surveillance footage inside the store once she figured out how to work her email."

Theo laughed from his desk and then cracked his knuckles.

"Sheriff. Deputy. Look away, please."

Chapter Fifteen

Wednesday evening as the sun melted into the horizon Kat drove down the county road to Puckett on her way back from a much-needed spa expenditure complete with a full body salt scrub, a mani-pedi, and had her roots touched up. The spa was relaxing and it helped to rid her body of anything pertaining to Brad.

After that, had taken her car in to be detailed. While Kat had waited for her car to be cleaned she took a moment to refresh her wardrobe. Out with the old and in with the new she thought as she checked the manicure that she had chosen and thought with a more professional shade of charcoal upon her return to the hospital.

She had to keep her feng shui balanced with her chakra thetan levels.

It was time for a change because next week she would be back on call and on the road and out of Carniville. There was something about Puckett that unsettled Kat. The town felt like a magnet and she was an iron sphere rolling towards it. Stuck in its inevitable pull.

She had one last night in that gold-fringed tissue box before she headed back to the city to restock her medical supplies and to receive her next charges for the week. *Maybe they'll send me to Idaho or Nebraska.*

What town would she be discharged to and where would she find Brad next? Hopefully, there would be better hotel selections and less pokey patrons.

She'd noticed that Deputy patrolling about incessantly whenever she took a walk around the park or even when she stepped out of the Unit to smoke. He was annoying, but he did have good taste in music. He was left there like some watchdog while the Sheriff was out patrolling the highways. There was no one at the Sheriff's Department either. The one-story Bavarian building had been empty.

She hadn't noticed any surveillance equipment and had peeped inside the front door and looked around. It looked more lived in than it did worked in and from the look of the action movie poster that hung on one of the four cell walls that's exactly what happened here.

The Sheriff and Deputy McGruff lived in the station. Together.

Don't people have social lives anymore?

Always working and never fully enjoying life. Taking life for granted as if time could be bought with the money earned.

Kat parked the Jaguar in front of Unit 10 one last time. She hated goodbyes, but she would certainly relish this one.

As Kat turned the knob of her Unit she heard footsteps behind her in the gravel. She jerked her body around to see Dick. The old man was in his pajamas as he walked towards her his face dark in the evening shadows.

The hemlines of his pants were soaked in dew from the grass and his pale feet were covered in clippings.

Dick Ballard wheezed as he caught his breath.

"I thought you had left, but I saw your headlights." He said in a whisper between breaths. He steadied himself against the motel wall shivering as his eyes locked onto Kat's and he took her hand in his.

"My Dorris, she's- I can't do it." Kat pulled him into her Unit and set him down in a chair. She grabbed his wrist and checked his pulse. It was dangerously high.

"Tell me what's wrong, Mr. Ballard. Is someone with Mrs. Ballard now?"

She attempted to comfort him, but instead, he sobbed and took her hand again in both of his trembling ones.

"She's in too much pain. I would end it for her myself, but I don't want to cause her any more pain. It's too much. She keeps moaning and complaining. She can't sleep. I can't sleep. I'm at my wit's end."

His head drooped and his liver-spotted hands shielded his face from Kat.

Kat looked at the time displayed on her phone's lock screen and then back at Dick. It was almost 7:30 PM.

"Okay, can you get back to Mrs. Dorris?" The old man nodded and listened intently to what Kat instructed him to do.

She had sent Dick Ballard back to his home to be with his wife while she packed up all of her belongings into her suitcases.

It was now 11:30 p.m., and she loaded up her car as quietly as she could. Then she cut across the grass and past the rusted teacup ride and rang the bell of the Pharmacy door. She heard its jingle inside the home and a hunched-over figure emerged from the shadowy doorway to permit her entry. She heard the muffled moans of Dick Ballard's wife as he gestured for her to follow as they walked through the empty Pharmacy shelves and through the living room where all of the furniture was packed in the room like sardines.

Dick and Kat entered the bedroom of Dorris Jean Ballard. Her walls were covered in pictures and family portraits dating back to when her father was a child. There were old picture books aged and open and stacked on top of each other on an antique desk. They must have spent days looking through those old pictures. The old memories of a time when they were young, virile, and carefree. A kinder time for them. One with less pain and heartache.

Dick walked to the side of the queen four-poster bed where his wife lay. Her twisted emaciated frame was enveloped by the rosebud-patterned quilt as she moaned in agony of the body that had grown to betray her.

"Everything is going to be alright, Dori. My love, your sweet nurse is here to help."

Dick placed his hand on his wife's and looked at Kat as he climbed into his side of the queen bed and lay beside her. Dorris moaned again from the sudden jostling of the bed and Dick Ballard wept once more as he stared at his wife.

Her eyes rotated to look at him from the corners as a tear slid down her gaunt cheekbone.

Kat walked to the table where Dick had placed the things she had requested. Rubbing alcohol, bleach, a towel, duct tape, and two trash bags. While Dick showed Dorris pictures from a worn photo album Kat poured the entire contents of the bottle of alcohol into the jug of bleach and then ripped the towel into shreds.

Dick was showing Dorris a picture as Kat walked over to Dorris's bedside. The elderly man gazed down at Kat's hands and his eyes pleaded.

"One moment- I just want to show her this one before-" His eyes darted back to the picture and a smile spread across his face as he turned the picture towards his wife and where Kat could also see it.

In the dim light, she could see that it was Dick Ballard and Dorris, just married and in love. A strapping Dick held a sultry young Dorris with dark locks by the waist as he lifted her in the air. Her beautiful smile was captured in sepia tones.

"Dori. Dorris, I have always loved you. Ever since I first saw you working at Floyd's, you were making malt milkshakes. I thought you were the most beautiful woman I had ever seen. When I look into your eyes now I still see her. My Dori."

He leaned over to kiss her on the lips tenderly and Dorris lifted her arm to rest on her husbands. An effort that caused her clammy brow to bead with sweat. Her head inched to the side where she could see her husband clearly. She breathed in a deep ragged breath.

"I love you, Dicky." Dorris struggled to say. He wiped the tears away and looked at Kat. He nodded and with a tremulous voice, he said.

Kat took the shredded towel, folded two strips into a square, and doused the terry fiber with the chloroform concoction.

Dick closed his eyes and began to recite Psalm 23 softly for him and his wife to hear. Her eyes intensely watched her husband from her peripheral vision with medicinally glazed eyes.

Her cracked mouth and parched tongue formed the words through the agony. Her inflamed jaw hinge rebuked it with every audible annunciation.

"Yea, though I walk through the valley of the shadow of death, I fear no evil: for thou art with me; they rod and thy staff they comfort me." He held his wife's hand in his and her feeble hand muscles gripped Dick's in hers.

"Surely goodness and mercy shall follow me all the days of my life: and I will dwell in the house of the Lord forever."

Tears streamed down Dorris Jean's gaunt features as Kat lowered the dampened wads of terry fabric over each of their noses. She held them firmly in place until their eyes that had stared into the windows of each other's souls closed one last time as Dick and Dorris Ballard began their journey to Heaven's door.

Kat hummed to herself as she then placed the plastic bags one by one over Dick and Dorris's heads, and peeled strips of duct tape to secure around their necks and to make them airtight. Kat would have preferred giving Dorris a double dose of morphine, but she had already given Dorris all that was in her medical bag as the elderly woman's tolerance to the stout medication had grown too high.

Kat had done this before in her days working in the hospital emergency room. She knew intentional wounds when she saw them enter through the automatic doors. Sometimes she was paid for her mercies and had it deposited into an account under Kathleen Walker to avoid any suspicion from the IRS as she assumed the identity of Kathy Walters.

An account was set up under the fundraiser she had organized for her old identities' search and rescue efforts. Kathleen Walker had up and vanished during the time her childhood home had gone up in flames. Everyone suspected she had done it since she had a track record for arson. But no one cared enough about the troubled teen that was Kathleen Walker or to search for the killer of Drunk Jim, so the fund went unused and had stayed stashed away for Kat's future retirement as it continued to accrue interest. A future retirement when she had finally taught Brad what it felt like to be used and abused for her sick amusement. She waited five minutes and watched as Dick and Dorris's chests rose and fell to a slower rhythm and the white plastic inverted *Thank You* bags clung tight to their features. The plastic impression created a synthetic smile on each of their obscured faces that spread from ear to ear.

Kat hesitated before leaving and took one last look at the elderly couple that lay motionless and curled towards each other in the bed. Two halves of a heart side by side and the picture book lay between them open to that same picture of Dick and Dorris in love like the couple in Helen Square. Their time-aged hands lay clasped together over the picture book and the two white envelopes addressed accordingly. Kat walked back through the living room and bumped into the Deputy who dropped his peanut butter and banana sandwich at her feet.

Chapter Sixteen

Bucky and Fiona lay wrapped up in each other's arms as they watched Forensic Files on the forty-nine-inch screen in Unit 5.

"You know you don't have to leave so soon when you are finished up here. You can hang around." Bucky said and his voice rumbled through his chest and tickled Fiona's ear. She smiled as she looked up from his bare chest. She rolled her eyes.

"Peaches, I know you are always on the road and working, but we could make things work." She sighed as she watched the investigators run a discovery on a poisoned victim.

"I just don't want to ruin a good thing. It always starts well." She sighed and traced heart shapes with her fingertips along the contour of his chest

"This time it could end well too. It's our turn for the universe to play in our favor. I work all the time too, so it wouldn't be like we'd trip over each other's feet. We understand that about each other. I love you, Fiona Peach. I love everything about you." He said in a low throaty voice.

Fiona pushed herself up on her elbows to look Bucky in the eyes. Her blushed nipples grazed the satin sheets. He had to be kidding. It was just like Bucky to try to push the relationship too fast. Mrs. Dorris had always told her that love comes softly and it was patient and kind and Bucky barrels in blind and never checks the corners of the room.

"Buck, I love you too. I do, but what if it doesn't?"

Bucky looked into her bright blue eyes and started to answer when they heard a commotion outside the motel. Their heads whipped towards the window and Bucky leaped out of the bed stark naked and ran to it. He pulled back the curtains and looked out the window, but couldn't see anything. However, the ruckus continued and grew louder as he searched for his boxers and holster. He heard car doors slam as he rushed to slip on his boxers and buckle his holster around his hips snugly.

Sheriff Bucky Ballard threw open the Unit's front door as he saw a flash of red amidst the rain of white gravel and the plumes of dirt that clouded his view. Bucky saw the dimmed glow of red taillights through the haze of dirt that headed in the direction of the school. On bare feet, he bolted across the street to the community center where his Charger was parked, and jumped in the driver's seat. He flipped on his squad car's siren and lights and burned rubber as he took off in the direction of the County Road that lay past the Little Red Schoolhouse and opened up to the Russell Scenic Highway 348.

As his car roared through the quiet streets of Puckett, Bucky saw the dust from the dirt gravel roads that rose high above the treeline. The vehicle ahead was booking it despite the hazardous roads and threat of sliding in the gravel as it surged forward and Bucky followed behind consumed by the vortex of the dirt storm that spewed from the four Pirelli's in front of the Charger.

The tree line that framed the road wound along the ground like a serpent along the mountain ridge as Bucky trailed the taillights ahead. Stray rocks connected with the Chargers windshield and across the hood and then the road spit them out onto the highway.

Once the vehicles exited the dusty gravel road and raced along the asphalt Bucky could see the car and who the taillights belonged to and it made Bucky's heart pound deep in his chest. The killer had gotten Kathy Walters and carjacked her Jaguar. His Aunt Dorris came to mind for a minute and the care Kathy Walter's provided for her in her time of need. The crimson Jaguar was headed Northwest towards State Highway 180 and the black Charger was hot on its tail.

The Jaguar F-type grew smaller and smaller ahead of him as Bucky reached for his walkie and touched a bare thigh. He had run straight out of the Cowrock without his cell and official walkie. He cursed as he fished in the passenger seat for Bus's walkie and without removing his attention from the road.

The walkie was out of reach until they turned onto 180 headed West where the force of the turn at such speed rolled the walkie into Bucky's grasp.

He brought up the walkie to his mouth as the Jaguar veered off suddenly onto Federal Highway 19 and he swerved to make the junction in the direction of Lover's Gulch. The Charger fishtailed on the loose asphalt, but with peak precision and skill Bucky handled the wheel in high-speed pursuit. He thumbed the PTT button and called out to Bus on his walkie.

If he could get in touch with Bus, then Bus could get a call out to dispatch.

"Bus. Pick Up. Over." He called over and over again as the charger gained on the Jaguar.

"Bus. Pick up. Over." He called, again, and again. The Jaguar ahead swerved to miss an opossum crossing the road. Bucky mirrored the crimson vehicle and darted into the left lane. The Charger lined back up with the Jaguar as they reached top speed in the center of the highway.

"Bucky?" Came Fiona's unsteady voice from the walkie.

"Fiona? Where's Bus? Why isn't he answering?"

"He's not with you? His cart was parked in front of your Aunt and Uncle's. He's not here, but-" Fiona's voice trembled and then went silent.

"What?" Bucky's voice raised higher under the intensity of the situation.

His brain couldn't comprehend what Fiona said to him as he focused on the road going at breakneck speed.

"Bucky, they're gone." Fiona's wracking sobs emitted from the walkie-speaker as the channel faded in and out.

"What? I can't- You're breaking up, Fiona." Bucky called into the receiver

"Bucky the killer was here in Puckett the whole time. We can't find him."

Fiona's voice continued to talk to Bucky in fast forward while the Jaguar ahead slammed on the brakes. The Jaguar came to a screeching halt and then took a sharp left down the trailhead that led to Lovers Gulch. He grabbed the walkie and hoped Fiona was paying attention. She had to get the call out, and Bucky had to make sure this murderer didn't get away.

Bucky raised the walkie to speak one last time.

"Fiona. Call in a report and have them dispatched to Lover's Gulch. Might need an ambulance too."

Bucky's Charger had narrowly missed the rear end of the Jaguar as it had dipped down the descending trail of Lover's Gulch. The squad car slid to a stop with its blue and red lights flashing in sequence to Bucky's heart palpitations. He bounded from the vehicle and left in the center of the highway. Fiona's disembodied voice carried out of the open door as he dashed down the trail.

"Bucky, wait for backup! Don't go-"

As Bucky's bare feet slapped the moist dirt, rocks, and litter along the trailhead he continued to regret not slipping shoes on, but time had been of the essence. If Bucky hadn't left when he had he would never have caught up to the Jaguar. He drew his gun from its holster and crept along the trail avoiding splintered trees, and broken glass from the side mirrors that had been taken off from trees along the sides of the trail. The trail had only been wide enough for two people to walk side by side, much less a car.

The trail opened up to the waterfall in the background and Bucky's eyes landed on the car. The front end hung haphazardly over the edge of the Gulch and its high beams cast sharp shadows across the area.

The driver's door of the Jaguar was wide open. Bucky's eyes scanned the area under the light of the moon above and the car's lighting granted. When he deemed it was clear, Bucky moved in slowly on the Jaguar. The car groaned against the rock's lip as it balanced like a top. He inched closer to see inside the Jaguar's cab, it was empty and a Cherry Pie scented 105.3 freshener hung from the rearview mirror. He heard footsteps up the trail behind him.

Bucky turned to face the sounds and saw Kathy Walters as she dashed up the trail.

"Kathy, Freeze!' Bucky shouted and Kathy stopped with her hands raised beside her head and turned around slowly.

"Explain yourself. What in the hell is going on here?" He said through shaking breaths and adrenaline.

"I don't know what you mean, Sheriff. I missed my turn back there. A chilly night, tonight?" Kathy Walters said nonchalantly as she quickly took a drag from the cigarette in her hand. She released a plume of smoke as she dropped the butt at her feet with the rest of the trash and ground it into the soil with the toe of her shoe.

Bucky ignored her lewd remark about his attire.

"Bullshit, and you know it. You are cutting out of town and my Aunt and Uncle are dead. You've been in their house. Sat at their table. Something's not adding up. What did you do? Did you leave a window open when you went to take a piss?" He kept his gun up and willed himself to settle on maiming her and then dragging her to justice.

"Fuck you, Sheriff. She wanted to die and you know it."

Kathy spat her words at Bucky. She glared at him as the mascara ran down her cheeks. Long-lasting and waterproof was never a bigger lie.

"You think you can just kill people and run off with no consequences. Is this what you do? Kill people for a living. I thought-"

"You thought. That's where you fucked up, Sheriff. What do you know about living? When do you do this living? You drive around the same circles every day, and for what? For who?" She stared at his hands which shook with rage as they held the gun pointed at her chest.

Open target and no cover, Kat was a fish in a barrel.

Bucky pointed at Kathy's figure that was outlined by the glare of the Jaguar's tail lights and bathed in a red glow. Kathy's features were devilish and wicked under the glare. Bucky ascended the trail slowly towards Kathy. She stiffened as he got closer and then he stopped. Bucky shifted sideways and kept his eyes and gun on Kathy. His face turned sheet white. He heard pounding and screaming coming from inside the trunk.

"Bucky!" He heard Bus's muffled shout.

He glanced back quickly at the Jaguar as it teetered over the side of the overhang as Bus moved around in the trunk. His breath caught in his chest and his heart hammered.

Bus couldn't tell where the car was at and that any wrong movement would throw off the weight distribution keeping the car from falling over the edge and into the Gulch below.

"Bus! I hear you! Don't move!"

Bucky returned his attention to Kat as she played Red Light, and Green Light and eased back closer to the trailhead away from Bucky and stopped when he looked back at her. She grinned like a Cheshire Cat that caught the canary bird as Bucky made his split decision.

Kathy understood the odds, it was her or Bus.

Bucky cursed under his breath, quickly holstered his gun, and then bolted to the Jaguar's open driver's side door. He pulled the release latch of the trunk lid. It swung high and the force of the trunk lid bounced open and the car rocked on its axis. Bucky glanced towards the trailhead as he rounded the car's rear and saw Kathy's form disappear at the top of the trail. He returned to Bus and removed the loose duct tape that had been over his mouth.

"Bucky, I'm glad to see you," Bus said relieved as Bucky leaned over the trunk. His hands were bound in duct tape and he spoke with a slur in his voice and seemed disoriented. Bus sat up in the trunk and Bucky felt his breath leave his body as Bus's eye widened.

The Jaguar groaned and lurched forward over the rock. The car's front lurched suddenly and the sudden force rolled Bus towards the backseat as the trunk slammed down and shut tight. When the trunk lid shut, the luxury car's bumper had connected vertically with Bucky's bare upper chest and jaw. It knocked him clear off his filthy feet and he came down on the flat of his back and laid there in a daze for a moment as he heard shouting. His vision flickered in and out. He shook his head and sat up and crawled across the rock on his hands and knees. He looked over the edge to see Jaguar as it slowly sank into the Gulch.

Bucky could see within the illumination of headlights and taillights as the Jaguar's cab filled with water. The trunk began to submerge beneath its warm temps. The Gulch water bubbled intensely around the crimson vehicle's frame as it inched deeper beneath the water. His vision dimmed as he saw flashing lights all around him and heard Fiona's voice.

Bucky woke up in the bed in Unit 5 at the Cowrock.

His memory was hazy as he sat up and looked around the room. Memories from the incident at Lover's Gulch were slowly coming back to him. The TV was muted and the news was on and Natalie was back on the scene again. She had red bumps up and down her legs and across her features that she had tried to cover with foundation and concealer. Crestburn's evening walk in the woods to the murder scene hadn't gone so well.

Bucky saw Lover's Gulch in a wide pan. Cut scenes of prior footage of the Jaguar submerged under the water. Interviews with people in the area who didn't have a clue what was going on, but Natalie loved the turmoil and to stir the pot. One long still image of the second murder scene. The empty pit in the ground surrounded by white pine trees would have the viewers glued to their screens to find out more grisly details. Natalie's views depended on the discord that boosted her ratings to the top of the charts.

Officials over the crime scene wove around the reporter as she silently mouthed the words of her inside report.

Bucky leaned over to the nightstand where the remote lay and his head spun and chest seared white hot. He grabbed the remote, settled back against the gold satin pillows, and then unmuted the TV as Detective Misquera stepped up beside Natalie. His normally dermaplaned complexion was covered in mosquito bites like his counterpart who spewed exaggerations from both corners of her forked tongue.

Looks like they went to the crime scene after all.

"Detective Misquera, can you give the viewers and me a statement, please? Are there any new updates in this investigation? It's been two days since this tragedy occurred. What are your thoughts on the investigation and do you have any words for the culprit?"

Natalie held the mic up to Detective Misquera. The Colombian stood like a great peacock as he fanned his feathers for the viewers. The corner of his mouth curled into a firm grin across his chiseled jaw. He stared dead into the camera's lens and the souls of the viewers.

"'Chu are probably watching thees. If 'chu are. I promise thees to 'chu. We will find 'chu and 'chu will pay for the lives 'chu 'ave taken."

Bucky rolled his eyes and muted the TV again. Whenever Misquera was on camera he suddenly became two hundred and one percent more Columbian and his accent thickened to near indistinguishable.

Pretty odd for a guy born in Chicago with parents from Wisconsin.

He laid against the pillows and stared at the popcorn ceiling as his mind ran through the events from two days ago if Natalie was accurate as she claimed on screen.

The door of the unit opened and sunshine spilled through the door and seared Bucky's sensitive retinas.

"Oh, you are awake. Finally, good to see you coming around. We've been worried about you." Came Fiona's voice as she walked in and shut the sun behind the wooden door.

That's when Bucky noticed the flowers sitting on the card table in the corner and several Get Well Soon balloons that floated against the tiny plaster stalactites that formed the ceiling above.

Bucky tried to raise up again and his pectoral muscles refused, but Bucky was persistent.

"Nope. You better just lie there and rest. You have a cracked sternum and mild concussion. You are lucky."

"What do you mean I'm lucky? Where's Bus." Concern seeped into his voice.

He saw her expression change to grim. She sat beside Bucky on the bed and held his hand.

"The force of that fall was enough to kill someone and once it hit the Gulch the trunk had filled with water. By the time we got to Bus, he was in rough shape. Aside from the broken legs, arm, and neck, he almost drowned."

Bucky's heart raced and then relief washed over him.

"Almost. Where is he at?"

"He is in traction in Unit 1 resting or more than likely eating ice cream and watching Law and Order. Maryanne has been more than helpful and has catered to Bus's every beck and call. He is in hog heaven despite the circumstances."

She forced a smile and then it slipped away and she looked at Bucky with swollen eyes from tears.

"Your Aunt and Uncle. She killed them." She said with venom in her voice.

"She did. She said she did."

"You saw her and let her go?"

"Of course not. It was her or Bus and the trunk opened and threw it off balance and it fell into the Gulch. I don't remember anything after that."

Bucky rubbed his weary eyes and scratched his head. Despite his vertigo, Bucky threw the covers back and stood up. He swayed sideways and then steadied himself as he marched to Unit 1, regardless of Fiona's effort to keep him on bed rest. He had to see Bus for himself.

Bucky shoved the unit's door open and shielded his eyes from the sun as he walked along the wall like a blind man he felt for 4, and 3, and 2, and bingo, Unit 1.

He opened the door slowly and saw Bus sitting up supported by a dozen gold satin pillows in an identical gold queen bed as the others in each Unit of the Cowrock. Bus watched Law and Order on his forty-nine-inch screen and ate Rocky Road ice cream with his uninjured hand. Bus also sported two full-length leg casts, an arm cast and sling, and a neck brace. Eye hooks above had secure slings that held his broken appendages in position improved blood circulation and promoted the healing process.

When Bus noticed Bucky he turned and Bucky saw all of the bruises that spread across his younger cousin's face, neck, and any exposed flesh. He was in rough shape indeed, but the mere sight of his cousin alive was a blessing. He had never wanted Bus to get involved with the cases, but he had.

The Deputy's eyes lit with a prideous flame as he saw the person he admired the most.

"Hey, Bucky!" Bus called and waved him over with his free hand.

"Hey, Bus. How are you feeling?" He asked and the Deputy laughed and swung his casted legs on the pulleys and counterweights.

"He's had loads of Tramadol and Morphine. He can't feel a thing."

Fiona said as she leaned with her arms crossed and her back against the open doorway. She watched the cousins as they interacted with a half-smirk on her face.

Bus scooped a spoonful of the Rocky Road with his left hand piled high with whipped cream and sprinkles into his mouth and grinned ear to ear.

"The nurse said I got the good stuff," Bus exclaimed through a mouthful of cream, nuts, and marshmallows. He was definitely feeling the effects of the medication cocktail.

"What nurse?" Bucky asked anxiously as he looked at Fiona.

"Not *that* nurse. She's a Lithuanian nurse. They brought the Feds in now. Once Theo retrieved the CC footage at the Jerry Jenrals through the IP address of the store's office computer system."

Fiona gestured to the ladder-back chairs at the coffee table and moved flowers, treats, and balloons as she discussed the case's updates since Bucky's medical hiatus.

"Theo found more footage on Kathy Walters through the system than what the Supervisor at Jerry Jenrals was attempting to send through an email."

"Yeah, a lot more. Amazes me still that in eighty-three years since the invention or reinvention of the computer people don't understand how to compress a file."

Theo stated with some residual annoyance at the computer-illiterate general store supervisor. Bucky hadn't even noticed Theo as he sat in a chair on the other side of Bus's gurnied bed as he too watched Law and Order over the top of his laptop screen.

"She was there then? Kathy killed Aaron Michaels too?"

The somber Forensic investigator nodded and Bucky put his face in his hands and tried to wake himself up from this recurring nightmare he'd been sucked into when he showed up to the Lover's Gulch scene.

It still didn't make sense.

He'd met her and she had cared for Aunt Dorris and then killed her and Uncle Dick, and almost took Bus with them.

Almost. The one two-syllable word that hung in his mind. He had almost lost Bus too.

"Josef Verderben, a local immigrant from Germany. Thirty-six. Five foot seven and one-eighty on the scale. Worked at a local butcher shop in the Alpine Village in Helen. The owner said Josef never came in on Monday and hadn't seen him since last Saturday." Randy divulged as he rested his forearm against the doorframe and looked around the room of battered and mournful faces, and Theo.

"So we know who Kathy Waters' victims are and their locations. She did it, but where is she now? If everyone showed up when I went unconscious no one saw her running away?" Bucky asked, exasperated by the continuous influx of information surrounding this case.

"Yeah, that part we have figured out," Fiona affirmed from the other ladderback chair and poked around the room.

"But the Feds are here now? Why?"

"They are here because once Theo sent in our full analysis of the reports on both crime scenes they matched up with a slew of other murders scattered about the United States. Niagara Falls for one."

More murders? Not just the four lives she took in White County? More.

Bucky's brain swam around like a big fish in a tiny bowl. Kathy Walters was a cold-blooded serial killer. He began to ask another question when Fiona interrupted.

"No more about the case for now. You need to rest."

"Also," Randy said from the doorway as he stepped into the room.

"You and Bus need to read these. I've already swabbed for fingerprints and got nothing back, but your Uncles." Randy handed a white envelope to both Bus and Bucky.

Inscribed on the envelope's face in Dick's scribbled writing was one word that read "Bucky" and he felt safe to assume that Bus's was addressed to Ballard's only biological son as well.

"I do need them back when you get finished reading, and before you open them, if you will put these on and try not to get anything on them. Just need to fingerprint them. I am sorry for both of your losses. Not trying to diminish the moment."

Fiona scowled at Randy as he retreated to the door.

Everyone quieted and glanced around the room at each other and then one by one Randy, Fiona, and even Theo, got up to leave the Unit.

Fiona kissed Bucky on the cheek before she left them to their privacy. Bus looked at the white envelope in his hand.

"Bus." He said aloud and looked over across the room at Bucky who flipped his own thin, white rectangle around in his hands.

Bucky stood with much effort as with each breath he felt barbs of pain spread like spider webs through his chest. He winced as he pushed the ladder back to Bus's bedside and then took a seat.

"Would you read mine out loud too, Bucky?"

"Are you sure Bus? I can open it for you."

"No, I want you to read it too. I never had a brother until you came along. I hate what happened to your parents and I hate feeling this way. I feel guilty because when you became my brother was the best day of my life." He knew Bus said it from his heart and that before he had ever come to Puckett, Bus had never been sociable with any other children. He had simply stayed in his room, listened to the radio, and forgone any social interaction.

"Bus, I know what you mean. That was a long time ago. I don't even think about it much and that bothers me, but I don't want you to dwell on that either."

"I'll dwell if I want to Bucky. All I've ever wanted is to be like you. To be you. You got it all.

236

You're tall and good-looking. Everybody depends on you."

"What do I have, Bus? A life of heartache and failed attempts."

Kathy's voice rang in his ears and his head swam in circles. Circles like he drove around in day-in and day-out.

"You don't even know it. Bucky, I know you care about me, but you don't see me the way everybody else sees me. Everybody thinks I'm a retard and I don't know anything. I hear them laughing behind my back at Floyd's and calling me chink eyes. I'm not even Asian."

"Who did?"

"It doesn't do any good, Bucky. It won't change anything. Like you always say Bucky, I can't hold their words in my hands. They don't mean nothin'." He nodded and looked ahead at the TV screen,

"I don't know Bus, you seem like a hero to me. I don't even know what happened. You were there before I got there." Bus looked back at Bucky.

"Yeah, but if you didn't try to save me you could have got her."

I failed again.

Bus was right. If he hadn't let his emotions get in the way he could have stopped Kathy. He hadn't been any help for Bus and it nearly cost him his life too.

"But that's okay, Bucky. Because Fiona will track her down."

"I know she will. It was what she was born to do. She was born to hunt down monsters like Kathy Walters that take people's lives into their own hands."

Bus looked at Bucky with concern and muted his TV.

"Let's see what these envelopes got in 'em. C'mon, Bucky."

"Mine or yours?"

"Do mine first."

Bucky's stomach lurched as he looked at the two envelopes in his grasp he carefully opened the one addressed to "Bus" with his purple gloved fingers and removed the folded sheet inside.

Chapter Seventeen

In the scribbled and shaky handwriting of Dick Ballard, Bucky read the words addressed to their one and only son.

"Bus the day you were born was a miracle in every way. Shortly after we were married, we were told by doctors that your mother would never be able to have children. But we prayed every night and every morning to God to send us one of his angels and that we would love that angel and never let him want for anything.

When we had almost given up Dorris got sick at the diner from all of the food smells and couldn't work. We thought she was ill and had rushed to the doctor in Helen to find out your mother was pregnant. What a joy and a blessing the news of your presence was in Puckett.

Back then Puckett was alive with people, games, and full of the laughter of children. It had been torture over the years wishing for a baby and hearing and seeing them all around. But then you were sent to us and our lives had just begun.

Dorris got extremely sick during the beginning of her last trimester and had to stay in the hospital. They informed us due to the circumstances and Dorris developing preeclampsia so early on in her pregnancy that there was a chance that you would not live through the term. Medicine then isn't what it is now, but we prayed that God would be in the hands, hearts, and minds of doctors and nurses.

You entered this world on February 2, 1990. You were perfect. Ten fingers, ten toes, and healthier than expected. We always knew you would be special and you were. We enjoyed watching you grow up and become a fine Deputy and a wonderful son. Everyone faces their disadvantages in life, Bus and you were born with a gift, not a curse. A gift people take for granted. God created you with a smile on your face and joy in your heart. You are a mirror for society, Bus. You show people and see people for who they truly are, no curtains drawn on your accomplishments. When the kids bullied you in school you never backed down. When your mother needed help and I was too busy with the Pharmacy you were there for her. When the Scout leader told you it would be okay if you didn't get all the badges, but you stuck to it and became an Eagle Scout. You are more than any condition you were labelled with and don't forget that.

Your Mother and I love you. We always have."

Bucky and Bus looked at each other with grief-stricken expressions.

Bus's eyes watered and fat tears streamed down his swollen and bruised face and dripped onto his neck brace.

He sniffled and scooped up a spoon of partially melted ice cream from the bowl and shoved it in his mouth.

He turned to Bucky, emotion thick in his voice.

"Yours, now."

Bucky carefully folded the paper back up and reinserted it into the envelope and put it aside for Randy to pick up. He felt awkward thinking Randy would probably read it and it would be filed with evidence. The big goldfish in the tiny bowl swirled in his head.

Bucky felt like he was having an out-of-body experience. He was over in the corner of the room, with his back to the ceiling as he watched himself slide an index finger under the paper seal and free the same notebook paper stationary, thirty-two lines, front and back from the envelope's mouth. He could see himself with his bandaged chest and swollen jaw as he looked at the letter written in the identical hand, albeit with more errors, markouts, and corrections. He had been in a hurry while writing it.

Bucky had seen his Uncle's handwriting more than anyone's at the pharmacy and every initial on pill bottles when he had helped fill in at the Pharmacy back in the days so long ago. Bucky cleared his throat as his eyes had already read preemptively into the letter before his tongue had a chance to wet itself.

"There aren't enough good men left in this world Bucky, and it was your mother's and my pleasure to have had the honor of raising you as our son. That's what you were to us. Not a nephew, a son.

Had I known that Dolly and Richard had led such deviant lives I would have intervened sooner. But that's what happens when a family moves away from each other and loses touch with one another. I truly thought I knew my brother better than that and I apologize. One's parents should never do such things to their children. I thought our parents had instilled a greater virtue within me and my siblings, but I was wrong.

Despite all of your shortcomings and the obstacles thrown your way, Bucky, you have broken that cycle for many families in this area.

Your mother and I know you've thrown your entire life on the back burner to do your duty every day and no one commends you on your sacrifices.

Good men go through Hell, Bucky, but they are the ones who discover what life is all about. You will. Dorris and I have been holding on to a secret for years because of a promise and that promise will not die with us.

Puckett was once owned by Howard Donald the illegitimate son of a mistress of Jeremiah Puckett's, the man who founded the town in 1910. Howard kept the town and fair running, but he was a sick man. He dropped by the diner one night when Dorris was closing up and took advantage of her. She came home sobbing and told me what happened. I marched outside and hunted him down and I killed Howard Donald in cold blood.

I did and I hope God forgives me for such a sin, but I knew Dorris would never rest soundly with Howard alive and breathing. I did what I had to do and I weighed his body down and threw it in Lover's Gulch and hoped it would wash away under the mountain.

When I saw on the news that skeletal remains had been found with the recent body discovered in the Gulch I knew my time was soon to be up.

I also knew with that discovery that you would never rest until you found out the truth behind it.

I realized this and would never want to put more weight on your shoulders to bear. I apologize again for choosing now to tell you all of this and not in person, but we felt it our burden to bear, yet in the end we felt we had better fess up than leave you to pick up the pieces. I knew that if I turned myself in then it would put everyone out and I couldn't handle the visits through plexiglass windows and two-way phones. I couldn't put that on any of you.

Michael Allen Donald, Howard's son, has embezzled the town dry and not reinvested into infrastructure so the fair died along with his father. That being said I want to leave you with these last words of mine as your father, not your uncle, or guardian.

Go live your life, son. Puckett's not all there is, there's more. And Fiona. Always such a nice girl. Just like our nurse.

She did what she thought was right and merciful. She has been incredibly kind to Dorris, but she could only do so much to ease her pain. The hospital had denied our request for a higher dose of morphine. They won't issue a higher dose of pain meds or her breathing would slow too much. The cancer went undiagnosed for so long it was beyond treatment. The meds only help so much. I have asked her to help your mother's pain go away.

Now, I don't want her to be in any trouble, because we both wanted this and she promised it would be painless. Painless is what Dorris needs.

No more pain.

No more hunger.

No more sleepless nights.

Only rest.

We are not afraid and we are of sound mind.

When I am afraid I put my trust in You. In God, whose word I praise-in God I trust. I will not be afraid. We may be buried soon, but our souls will not be there. Live your life, Bucky, and enjoy it. It goes by so fast. Forgive me for my faults, Bucky, I am only a man and I did what I thought was right and in your mother's honor and for our family's. You have a good head on your shoulders and Bus is more capable than you believe him to be. Take care of each other.

We love you, Son.

And below Dickard Ballard's signature was a PS.

"Safety deposit key is in the bowl on the shelf between your portraits."

Bucky exhaled a breath he didn't realize he had been holding in.

He couldn't fully wrap his head around the information.

Bus wiped his eyes on the back of his hand.

"I can't believe they are gone." He released his pent-up sigh.

"I know Bus. Me either." Bucky agreed as he rested his elbows on his knees and stared at the letter in his trembling hands. He willed the tears that dripped down his face to cease, but they flowed free shackles of his tear ducts. He had always tried to be strong for Bus whenever life threw him a curveball in the teeth. He chose to smile through the pain, but they both soaked up the closure the letters provided. They hadn't gotten to say goodbye and the letters gave their broken hearts some relief. She wasn't in pain anymore and Dick didn't have to live without the love of his life. Bucky had always been too busy to stop in and visit during the days or nights. There had always been other priorities and the Ballard's, his parents, had understood.

"They asked the nurse to do it. She helped Momma."

"But she still took their lives, Bus. She can't do that. She doesn't have the right to end someone's life. Even if they asked her to do it. Kindness doesn't change the law and she's killed dozens of others too. Not just them. Not just old people who wanted to die."

Bucky's voice raised an octave higher and harsher than he had intended and Bus shrunk in his bed.

"I know." The Deputy said quietly as they sat together in silence soaking in the two letters.

A knock on the door sounded and Bucky permitted entry. Fiona opened the door a crack and then came in with Randy behind her two evidence baggies in hand. He stopped in front of Bucky and held the bags open and the Sheriff deposited the envelope in each one.

Randy then hurried out the door and back to the community center.

Fiona stood behind Bucky and rubbed his back shoulders, slid her arms around his neck softly, and whispered into his ear.

"It's getting late. I think you could use some rest. You need a break."

Her words tickled the goldfish's fin as he turned to her.

"Peaches, I'll rest when I'm dead." He smirked.

Fiona snickered and kissed him on the scruff of his cheek.

"Can you hand me my radio, please ma'am?" Bus interrupted.

Fiona picked the battery-operated radio off of the dresser and handed it to Bus and then flopped down in the chair across from Bucky. Bus tuned his radio to 105.3 as Bucky and Fiona stood up to leave the Unit to go to their own for some privacy.

Fiona touched his bruised jaw with her fingertips. "Soo lucky you didn't break your jaw."

"I don't feel lucky, but at least I'm in better shape than Bus." The Deputy was completely focused on his radio and getting the station to come in.

The tuner jumped between songs and faded in and out until he hit the sweet spot and the static hissed out the melody.

"I can take your breath away. I can be your hero."

When the channel came in clear and the song ended they heard a deep based frequency erupt from the mono stereo speakers as the Love Doctor returned from a short intermission break to take his patients.

"That was *Iglesias's Hero*. Call into the Love Doctor and let me soothe those aching hearts tonight. Let's try this again. Last chance of the night before I sign off. Gotta get up bright and early for that dentist appointment."

The tiny speakers rattled under the bass of the Love Doctors' chuckle. Although the Love Doctor was smooth as the sheets on the beds at the Cowrock, Bus noticed a slight twinge of irritation in the disc jockey's voice.

"I don't know how you all listen to late-night radio. I like music and all, but sheesh, throw something informative in there to liven it up a little."

Fiona covered her ears and Bus turned the volume down some to appease the crowd.

"Let's see who's on the line this time. Who is my last caller? Who is caller no. 5?"

The Love Doctor said in the background as Bucky pointed out Fiona's fascination with listening to people talk for hours on end, but the material was different. It was about serial killers and cold case files, not pop culture or scripted mediated discussions about music and local politics.

"Hey, LD, it's me. Again." A voice giggled over the airwaves and Bucky and Bus stiffened as the caller trilled a greeting to the Love Doctor.

"It's *her*. That's *her* voice."

Bus said and his cast enveloped legs swung wildly. That voice instantly sent chills down his spine as he remembered the acrid taste and smell of bleach and rubbing alcohol in his nose. He grew nauseous as his olfactory senses went into overdrive and the meds and dairy were at war with his stomach.

"It sounds just like her," Bucky exclaimed and sat up straight in the chair to hand Bus a small trash can from beside the bed. He winced and sat back as his muscles and bones rebelled against his sudden movements and recoiled in his chair.

Fiona stood up and rushed to Bus and Bucky.

"*Sugar* is Kathy Walter's?" Fiona asked exasperatedly as she held the trash can in one hand and rubbed Bus's neck as he vomited an entire rocky road into the receptacle.

"That's her alright," Bus said through retching.

"I've heard of her there before. She calls in every night that The Love Doctor is on call. Always hoggin' the line.

I thought her voice sounded familiar when I bumped into her."

Bus then dry heaved and produced nothing. He sat for a moment as he caught his breath as Fiona wiped his face clean with one of the motel's burgundy washcloths. She then went to tend to Bucky as he doubled over and held his chest through the spiderweb of fiery needles in his chest.

"I'm alright. I'm alright." Bucky swatted away her hands.

"Are you positive that Caller No. 5 is Kathy Walter, Bus?" She stared at the battery-operated

FM radio that sat in Bus's golden lap as the female voice spoke to the Morgan Freeman of late-night talk radio. The voice of the night.

"Does a bear shit in the woods?"

Epilogue

The white Bic lit up the tobacco on the tip of Kat's Virginia Slim as she drove along the spine of the Blue Ridge Mountains. Music and voices wailed through static from the stereo of the beat-up Cadillac Seville she had hot-wired at a car dealership in Owltown.

The GPS on her prepaid phone stated in robotic tones that there were eighty-nine miles left in her destination. She swiped the banner message up and pressed the call button and the phone line rang openly.

"Hello, you are Caller No. 5. What pain can the Love Doctor take away tonight? What's your name? Where are you from? What's your story?"

"Hey, LD. It's me, again." Kat giggled as she spoke over the wind that streamed in through the rolled-down driver's side window. Her phone perched on her cracked-up dashboard clasped in a holder with the 105.3 *The Love Line* logo shined like a beacon as the GPS banner popped up to make the next exit.

"Sugar, now I don't want to have to tell you again. You have called in every night and I appreciate the support, but you have taken up each position in place tonight. We need to share a little with the rest of the listeners. Too much Sugar isn't always a good thing." The Love Doctor struggled to keep an even sultry voice for the invisible audience.

"But I want to see you, LD," Kat said in a childish voice.

The boys in the back whooped and hollered.

"Oh, you do?" He gave a deep throaty chuckle across the airwaves.

Kathleen Walker took a long drag of her Virginia Slim.

"Oh, yeah. I need a doctor."

Made in the USA
Columbia, SC
26 September 2024

43034014R00152